New York Times bestselling author **Maisey Yates** lives in rural Oregon with her three children and her husband, whose chiselled jaw and arresting features continue to make her swoon. She feels the epic trek she takes several times a day from her office to her coffee maker is a true example of her pioneer spirit.

Also by Maisey Yates

Gold Valley Vineyards

Rancher's Wild Secret
Claiming the Rancher's Heir
The Rancher's Wager

Copper Ridge

Take Me, Cowboy
Hold Me, Cowboy
Seduce Me, Cowboy
Claim Me, Cowboy
Want Me, Cowboy
Need Me, Cowboy

Discover more at millsandboon.co.uk.

Rancher's Christmas Storm

MAISEY YATES

MILLS & BOON

First published in Great Britain 2021
by Mills & Boon, an imprint of HarperCollins*Publishers* Ltd,
1 London Bridge Street, London, SE1 9GF

www.harpercollins.co.uk

HarperCollins*Publishers*
1st Floor, Watermarque Building,
Ringsend Road, Dublin 4, Ireland

Large Print edition 2021

Rancher's Christmas Storm © 2021 Maisey Yates

ISBN: 978-0-263-29324-1

10/21

One

As Honey Cooper looked around the beautiful tasting room that—other than the vineyards themselves—was the crown jewel of Cowboy Wines—she thought to herself that if she had a book of matches and just a tiny bit more moxie, she might've burned the entire place to the ground.

Not that it could ever be said that she was lacking in moxie—maybe it was just the desire to avoid prison. Perhaps not the best reason to avoid engaging in the torching of her family winery. Scratch that, her family's *former* winery.

Until it had been sold to Jericho Smith. Jericho Smith, who was the most infuriating, obnoxious, sexy man she had ever known.

He made her itch. Down beneath her skin where she couldn't scratch it. It drove her crazy. And now he had her legacy. Just because her brothers were no longer interested in the day-to-day running of Cowboy Wines and her father wanted to retire, Jericho had offered to buy and her father had sold. Sure, she had a tidy sum of money sitting in her bank account that her father had felt was her due post sale, but that didn't matter. It wasn't the point.

Maybe she should go find a matchbook.

Instead, she looked down at her phone— she had bought herself a smartphone with her ill-gotten rage money—and saw that it had lit up again. She had a message.

It was from Donovan. Which thrilled her a little bit.

Donovan ran an equine facility up north, on

the outskirts of Portland. She had met him on a dating app. A dating app. Yes, Honey Cooper had signed up for a dating app.

But the thing was, she was really sick of the pickings down in Gold Valley. She was sick of cowboys. She was sick of everybody knowing her brothers. Her father.

Jericho.

She was untouchable here. They might as well up and put her in a glass case. Everybody acted like they were afraid of getting punched in the face if they came within thirty yards of her. In fairness, they probably were in danger of getting punched in the face. Jackson and Creed weren't exactly known for their measured temperaments, and when it came to Jericho… Well, he was the older brother that she absolutely didn't need.

He twisted her up in ways she hated, and had for as long as she'd noticed that boys were different from girls. Of course, the problem with knowing a man that long was that he could only see you as the pigtail-wearing brat you'd once been and would never really see you as a woman.

There was also the fact she knew all too well that Jericho's personal policy when it came to relationships was that they were best as a good time, not a long time.

But he was just so hot.

So was Donavan though. You know, if the pictures that she had gotten from him weren't a lie. No, they weren't those kind of pictures. He had not sent her his nudes. She wasn't sure if she was offended by that or not, as she had it on very good authority—TV—that men often sent women their anatomy when they wanted to hook up.

Not that they physically sent their anatomy, but pictures of them.

Still, she was on the road to getting out of Gold Valley, to getting away from the winery—without setting it on fire—and getting away from Jericho once and for all.

That was part of the problem. The proximity was killing her. She still lived at Cowboy

Wines. And she felt surrounded—absolutely surrounded—by her father's perfidy.

So she was going to run away to Portland. Take a job at a different ranch. Maybe lose her virginity to Donovan.

No, she was *definitely* going to lose her virginity to Donovan.

For Christmas.

And she would forget all about Jericho and the fact that she thought he was hot. And the fact that he had devastated her by buying the winery. The winery that had been her only dream, her only goal for as long as she could remember. She'd knuckled down and worked the land, worked it till her knuckles bled, the same as the rest of them, for years. And now it was gone.

To add insult to injury, she still thought he was hot. Even while furious with him. Even while he took a new woman into his bed practically every night. Which didn't matter.

She didn't care about that. She didn't care. Because she didn't actually want to date him. She just wanted to climb him like a tree.

And who didn't? Honestly. He was incredibly beautiful. Tall, broad and well muscled. Sin in cowboy boots. And in a cowboy hat. And a tight T-shirt. And as much as she would like to actually be sick of cowboys, it was kind of her aesthetic.

She'd lost her mother when she was only thirteen, and it had stuck with her. There was something about the loss that was a lot like the bottom of the world had fallen out, and she'd done her best to cling to what she could.

She had her dad, she had her brothers and the most important thing to her had been to fit in with them.

She knew that dealing with her in her grief had been hard for her dad so she'd done her best to be more stoic. She'd pushed off her desire to experiment with makeup or clothes or anything like that.

She'd become the cowgirl she needed to be.

But it hadn't gotten her anywhere. Now she was ready for something else.

To see what else she could do and be.

Donovan was different. He was sophisticated. The place he ran was an *equine facility*. It wasn't a *ranch*. She wouldn't be a ranch hand. She would be a horse trainer. She would be fancy. She would be free.

She would not be a virgin.

If her father didn't think that she needed a winery, then she didn't need to be around them.

That made her heart clench tight. She wasn't... She wasn't going to fall out with her family. Not entirely. Her mother had died when she was so young, and her father had taken good care of her. But he just didn't understand having a daughter. He loved her. She knew that—no matter how difficult things had been around the time of her mother's death, she did know that. But it didn't occur to him that she might want a piece of this place. Even though she had worked it most of her life.

And her brothers... They were pains in the butt. They really were. But they loved her. She needed distance though.

She so badly needed distance.

And she had a plan to get it.

She picked up her phone and looked at the message.

What's your estimated date of arrival?

I was thinking the week of Christmas.

She was actually thinking she'd leave tomorrow. That was what she was thinking. Leaving tomorrow. Getting out. Getting gone. Pulling off the Band-Aid.

She had never missed Christmas with her family before. But this was part of her defiance. She wasn't going to consult them on her leaving. She was going to just… She was going to go. She was going to do whatever she wanted.

She didn't need to ask their permission, and she hadn't. She hadn't told them any of what she was thinking, or let them know how furious she was, because why would she?

Her dad didn't want to deal with her emotions anyway.

Plus he was rarely around anymore. She had no idea what was going on with him, but he was never home. Her brothers were married now—and to the Maxfields at that. Which meant they would be off doing things at their fancy winery. Or worse. Expecting her to join them.

It wasn't that she didn't like her sisters-in-law. They were just…a lot. A whole lot. Cricket was her age—she supposed they ought to be friends. It was just… She had a difficult time thinking about how she was going to cozy up to a girl who was sleeping with her brother. *Ew.*

That would work just fine. I'll have a room ready for you.

She hoped that it would be a room *with* him.

She had to do something. To erase this place, her pain, her stupid, pointless attraction to Jericho, the man who had stolen her whole future from her. The man who owned way too much space in her head.

Her stomach twisted in defiance of that thought.

She did hope there was a room ready for the two of them to share. She *did*. She was ready. She was ready for this. For a change. For something new. For a chance to be different.

She was going to make her way in the world. And she did not need Cowboy Wines to do it.

Jericho was tired. Down to his bones. And he only had a day or so before he had to leave for the Dalton family Christmas.

He would love to resist it. Hell, he would love to be an asshole and just stay away entirely no matter how many times the Daltons reached out. But two months ago, he was contacted by West Caldwell, who was apparently his half brother, telling him about his connection to the Dalton family.

Apparently Hank had expected Jericho would be too mad to speak to him, considering it had come out that his various half children were under the impression he'd known about them and denied them, even though that wasn't true.

West had been the voluntary envoy, meeting him down at the Gold Valley Saloon, explaining the situation and how he himself had come to be in Gold Valley and come to be part of the Dalton clan.

The thing was, Jericho had already known about his connection to the Daltons. He'd known about it from the time he was old enough to understand that everyone had a father—it was just that his own didn't give a fuck.

But it turned out he'd gotten that wrong.

Hank Dalton hadn't known. The infamous retired rodeo cowboy was apparently the father to a whole passel of kids he didn't know he had. Owing to his wild years, when he had been philandering and cheating on his wife—and apparently not understanding condom usage—he had a spread of kids in their thirties. Some of whom were with his wife, Tammy, others of whom were not.

Apparently, he was the last one who hadn't been tracked down, owed to the fact that Hank hadn't known his first name, and his last name was so common.

Hank was infamous in Gold Valley, and his mother had made no secret of the fact that he was his father.

But then, his mother had died when Jericho was only sixteen, and it had been the Cooper family that had taken him in. Finished raising him. Made sure that he never wanted for much of anything.

Cancer was a bitch and it had taken his strong, caring mother from him far too soon. A pain he had in common with the Coopers. They didn't talk about it—feelings weren't high on their list of things to deal with—but they all just…knew. That was enough.

They'd been enough.

And he had just never… Hank had rejected her as far as she was concerned, and Jericho had never wanted to take a damn thing from Hank.

But the story was more complicated than

that. It turned out it was Hank's wife, Tammy, who had dealt with the former mistresses who'd all had his children. Hank himself had never really known.

And so he was... He was doing this. He was heading up to this family Christmas thing. And he didn't know what the hell was in store for him. But he'd spent his life without any real family. He was curious, frankly. To see this whole big family that was his.

Thankfully, Honey would be around to see to the running of the winery. Plus, Jackson and Creed could get their asses in gear to give them some help. They were like brothers to him.

And Honey was...

Under his skin in ways he didn't like to acknowledge. He'd known her since she was a scrappy, spiky kid, and now she was a scrappy, spiky woman who ignited his blood and made him question if hell was really all that hot, or if it was something he should risk.

Lord knew, if he ever touched her, Jackson and Creed would have his head on a pike.

And if he were the kind of man who could offer something extra, it might be different.

But in his mind, love was a sacrifice. And he'd bled out all that he could on that score.

So he kept his fly up and his hands to himself. Around her anyway.

Unwanted attraction aside, she was a good worker, and she would be more than up to the task of seeing to the place around the holidays. In fact, since he'd bought the place, he swore she'd been working two times as hard.

Being here without him wouldn't be that difficult either, especially because it wasn't exactly prime wine tasting time. They had a couple of private parties, but otherwise, people were getting together and sitting outdoors and watching music every week during this time of the year. Maybe his success in life was part of the reason he'd agreed to meet with the Daltons.

Because hell, he'd gotten pretty far in life without Hank.

He pulled himself up from nothing with bloody knuckles. Bought his first ranch after years of working it. Bought another one. Expanded. Made profits. Got to the point where he could buy the winery. And now he had several different business ventures relating to ranching and agriculture.

And he was successful. No matter how you looked at it.

He didn't need the Daltons' pity or their money. There had been a time when his mother really could've used it. They had gotten a single settlement from Hank, but her cancer had bankrupted them.

He'd been a kid left with nothing in the end. And yeah, he'd spent some time being bitter about it. Until he'd decided the best revenge could only ever be living well, and he'd done whatever the hell he could to make sure he was living as well as any man could be.

He worked hard, he played harder. Family, marriage… That shit wasn't in the cards for him.

He walked into the winery tasting room, to see Honey leaning over the table on her phone. She was wearing a pair of blue jeans that seemed on a mission to hug her ass as tightly as possible.

No. Honey was not his sister. She was also barely over the age of twenty-two, too damned young, too damned earnest and more likely to bite him on the wrist than kiss him. She was like a wild mink.

And damn if it didn't appeal.

He knew exactly when the switch had flipped, and he did his best to never think about it. It had been back last November when Creed had announced he was marrying his rival—because she was pregnant.

Honey had been incensed, a furious little ball of rage.

"You don't marry somebody just because you lust after them. That's silly."

"Fine. The pregnancy."

"I still don't understand how you could be so stupid. You're not a kid."

"Honey, I pray that you always keep your head when it comes to situations of physical desire."

"I would never get that stupid over a man."

She'd said that with total and certain confidence and something had broken inside him. Shattered. She was a woman.

And he wondered what sort of man could make her that stupid.

His immediate, gut response had been… *Him.*

He'd wanted to run out of there like his pants were on fire and his ass was catching. Instead he'd stayed—like it was nothing—and tamped it all down to a manageable burn.

It was what he'd been doing ever since.

"Afternoon."

She lifted her head slowly, then turned to look at him, her expression cool. "Jericho."

"Did you practice that face in the mirror?"

"What face?" she said, the coolness evaporating immediately, her eyebrows locking together.

"There you go. Now you look like you. I'm going to need you to oversee things while I'm gone over Christmas."

"Excuse me?"

"You heard me."

She blinked wide, whiskey eyes. "Do you think that you're my... Do you think you're my boss, Jericho?"

"Honey," he said, realizing that he was tempting fate. And her temper. "I own the winery now. You do work for me." He was the one that would be signing the checks once that first pay cycle ended. So maybe she hadn't realized it. But it was true.

"I... I quit," she said.

"Excuse me?"

"I quit. I'm leaving, actually. I'm leaving."

"You're leaving?"

"Jericho, do you always just repeat what women say? Because if so, I find it hard to believe that you have such good luck with them."

"Women don't gravitate to me for my conversational skills," he said.

A streak of color flooded her cheeks. And he would be a fool to read anything into that.

"I don't really care why women seek out your...company. I'm not seeking your company out. I'm leaving. I got a job."

"You..." He realized he was about to say *you got a job*. "Where?"

"Up near Portland."

"What are you going to do? Work at one of those assy coffee shops that only serves drinks in one size? And sells more macho than coffee?"

"It's not in the city. It's a ranch on the outskirts. An equine facility. I got a job there as a trainer."

"Sight unseen?"

"Yes."

"What the hell is this place called?"

"None of your business."

"Does your father know?"

"My father is too busy with... Well, he seems to have taken to my brothers marrying into the Maxfield family with a lot of enthusiasm."

"What's that supposed to mean?"

He knew what it was supposed to mean. Cash Cooper had carried on a youthful affair with Lucinda Maxfield years ago. Time and misunderstandings had separated them. But since her marriage to James had fallen apart, and Cash's wife had passed, he suspected the two of them had rekindled things.

And it seemed Honey suspected it too.

"Apparently the Maxfield women are universally irresistible to the men in my family." She shook her head. "But I don't want to spend my Christmas at Maxfield Vineyards. I don't want to be part of their fancy ass… whatever. I don't want you to own Cowboy Wines. I want everything to go back to the way it was. But it isn't going to. Which means I'm going to take myself off. I got a place. And I really like… I really like Donovan."

"Who's Donovan?" he asked, eyes narrowing. Jackson and Creed weren't currently in residence, which meant that it was up to him to make sure she wasn't doing anything dumbass.

Honey was open; she was honest to a near fault. If the thought was in her head, it was out of her mouth just as quick.

The fact that she'd been keeping secrets set off big loud alarm bells.

"He owns the equine facility that I'm going to," she said, sniffing loudly. "And I've been talking with him on an app."

His stomach went tight. "Explain."

"Well, if you must know, I met him on a dating app."

"You met a guy that you're going to go work for *on a dating app*?"

"Yes."

"This is an HR violation waiting to happen."

"I think he might be HR."

"All the more reason for you to turn tail and run. This doesn't sound like a safe situation at all."

"I'm not a *child*, Jericho. And anyway, I'm going up there with the express intention of violating HR mandates."

"Hell no." Anger burned in his gut. Honey might not be for him. He knew she wasn't. But even so, he was not going to let Honey Cooper run off up north to shack up with some guy who owned an equine facility—that was the most pretentious little bullshit he'd ever heard—and…start sleeping with him immediately. The very idea made him see red.

"No," he said. "You are not doing that. You are staying here."

"It may shock you to learn, Jericho, that you don't get to control my life. You don't get to tell me what to do. You don't even get the tiniest say in what I do with my time. Because it isn't your business."

"You are my business, Honey Cooper, whether you like it or not."

She rounded on him, her expression a fury. "You're not my brother, asshole. You're not my boss, and it isn't your decision. I'm leaving. I'm leaving tomorrow. I've got everything packed up."

"That's a problem, because I'm also leaving tomorrow."

"Sounds like a you problem."

"Honey…"

"No," she said. "I'm out. I should've been the first in line to buy the winery. My father never consulted me. You never considered it.

You never considered my feelings at all. Acting concerned for me now, when you bought out my family's winery without thinking that I might want to…"

"I didn't realize Cash didn't consult you." He felt slightly guilty about saying that, because Jackson had basically told him that Honey wouldn't be happy about the decision. And he'd chosen to ignore that. He'd chosen to go ahead with it, because it was what he wanted. There wasn't a whole lot in this world that he could claim as a legacy. His mother was dead; his father had never wanted much of anything to do with him—so he'd thought. Cowboy Wines was the closest thing he had to a family anything. The Coopers were the closest thing he had to a family.

Which meant that getting a piece of it had mattered to him. And when Cash had wanted out…

He never mentioned the possibility of selling it to Honey. It wasn't like he had taken it out from under her deliberately. And she hadn't said anything, not a damn thing, in the time since.

But Honey's happiness meant something to him. The Coopers meant something to him. Which was why, no matter how nice Honey's ass looked in a pair of jeans, he'd never do anything about it. There were plenty of women out there. More than willing to warm his bed for a few hours. He wasn't going to mess with his friends' sister. He also wasn't going to let her go off half-cocked to warm some other dude's bed just because she was mad.

Not that he didn't figure she'd be warming beds, or that she hadn't. It was just that this was a bad idea. Clearly, up front from the start. And there was no point doing something that was so clearly this dumbass right from step one.

"It doesn't matter whether you knew or not. You should talk to me. You all should talk to me."

"The thing is, I wanted it." He figured honesty was the best policy here. "Whatever was going to get it. Whether you're happy about it or not."

"Well, I'm not happy. But it doesn't matter, because I won't be around to be unhappy anymore. Fuck you."

She turned around and stalked out of the room, and he resisted the urge to go after her. Honey and her tantrums weren't his problem. He had bigger issues. Like making sure everything was covered before he went up to deal with the Daltons. Of course, if he called Creed and Jackson about it, he would blow Honey's operation. Which was probably for the best.

He took his phone out of his pocket and dialed Jackson. "Hey. I'm going to need your help with the winery for the next week."

"All right."

"I'm going to meet my family."

"Your family?"

"Yeah. My father. Hank Dalton."

"Well, hell."

"Don't say it like that. It's not that big of a deal."

"It *is* a big deal," Jackson insisted. "He finally acknowledged your existence?"

He didn't particularly want to talk about this. But it was reality right now, so he supposed there was no avoiding it. "He didn't know about my existence. Apparently."

"Hell."

"I don't see it as that big of a deal. So I don't see why you should."

"Because it's a big fucking deal."

"Only if you think I'm going to make a big, happy family out of it. I'm going up for some big Christmas thing. That's it."

"Well, I don't mind helping out." And he thought about selling Honey out just then. But he didn't.

"Thanks."

He might pay for that later. But he would deal with her. No point sending Jackson off after her.

She was already angry enough. He wouldn't make it worse. And hell, she would see reason. He couldn't actually imagine Honey taking off and moving up north. She wouldn't do it.

No. She would come to her senses and see reason.

She had to. He didn't want to think too deep about the alternative.

Two

Honey flung a suitcase into the bed of her truck and slapped her hands together. She had every box in her bedroom all packed up. And she was ready to go. She had left a note for her dad.

The boxes would be picked up by a moving company—she was really enjoying the fact that she'd gotten a bit of money from the sale of the winery—and driven up separately.

She would be taking her truck and an overnight bag. Traveling light. And she was ready. Especially after that discussion with Jericho yesterday. Which couldn't even be called a discussion. He was such a high-handed dick. And she was over it. Honestly, completely and utterly over men acting like they thought they knew what was best for her life. *If it was only acting like they knew what was best for my life, it wouldn't be that bad.* But they actually made decisions that impacted her life and didn't seem to get it when it infuriated her. More than infuriated. She was so... She was just so hurt by the whole thing with the vineyard.

She didn't know that she would ever really get over it.

Getting ready to leave this place now... She wished that it felt more triumphant. Instead, it felt sad. This place housed the few memories that she had of her mother. And so many happy ones with her father and her brothers. And yes, even Jericho.

They were a close family, and they always had been. But this move by her dad had driven such a wedge between them.

A wedge she hadn't told anyone about. But

she didn't know how. Didn't know how to do it without flying off the handle, and after a decade of keeping it all to herself, the idea of letting it all out terrified her.

And her brothers had gone off and got married… It was just that everything was different. She didn't think it could ever go back to the way it was. No, she knew it couldn't. So she might as well start over. She might as well.

She put her hands on her hips and looked back at the room that was neatly stacked with boxes and then looked at her truck. There was no point delaying it now. She was on her way.

She walked around to the other side of her truck and started when she saw Jericho standing back next to a tree, his arms crossed over his broad chest.

His black hat was pulled low over his face, his dark eyes glittering. "And where exactly do you think you're going?"

"Lake Oswego," she said.

"Oh please," he said. "You're going to last

about five minutes there. You're going to die of hipster."

"I don't think Lake Oswego is renowned for its hipsterdom."

He arched a dark brow and it made her stomach feel funny. "You're really leaving?"

She frowned deeply. "My shit is packed. What do you think?"

"Stay," he said, the word low and rumbling, and it tugged at her and she hated it. She had to get away from here. From him. She'd wanted a whole bunch of things for years. To be an equal to her brothers, to work this winery as they'd done and be able to have a piece of it someday. For Jericho to look at her with heat in his eyes. She wasn't going to be able to find new patterns if she didn't change things. Everything. "Don't be rash about it."

She really wanted to punch him for that. He had no idea. This wasn't rash. It was the culmination of so much stuff. Of realizing that she was going to be treading water in Gold Valley for the rest of her life.

She had no career here. Not like she'd believed.

Her crush—toxic attraction sprinkled with a dash of irritation… Whatever you wanted to call it, it was on him.

"I'm going to go."

"Look. I asked your brother to come here and handle things while I was away, and I did not blow your cover. So now I want you to be reasonable."

"*Reasonable* meaning do exactly what you want me to do?"

He lifted a brow, which she had privately deemed his most arrogant eyebrow some years ago. "Hell yeah."

She huffed. "Jericho, I don't owe you the reality that you want. You sure as hell didn't care about what I wanted when you bought the winery."

"It wasn't that I didn't care."

"It was. You didn't talk to me about it. Nothing. My entire world felt like it had been pulled out from under my feet."

"How is it different? You didn't own the

place when your dad ran it. Why is it so different working for me?"

"Because I…" It hurt, this admission. But she was going to have to practice it because she was going to have to tell her dad eventually. Tell him without dissolving. She might as well practice on Jericho. "Because I expected someday that maybe my father would leave this to me. To us. I don't have any problem with you having a piece of it. You've been part of us from… For a long time. But me being cut out of it…that's what I can't understand."

"You got some money."

"I did. But it's not the same as getting this land. I can go earn money anywhere. Which is what I'm going to do."

"And you're going to sleep with this guy?"

That spiked a wave of fury in her blood. He had her vineyard. He had her desire. He didn't deserve to be spared her honesty. "Yep. Lots of times."

"Honey…"

Her eyes collided with his, and there was

something about the look on his face that made a reckless heat careen through her blood. Because while she was talking about sleeping with Donovan, she couldn't actively picture it. Yes, she'd seen photographs of him, but they couldn't compare to Jericho standing in front of her in the angry, hard, hot flesh.

His mouth firmed into a grim line.

"What?"

"It's a bad idea," he said, his voice hard.

"So what?" she asked. "Has every one of your ideas been good?"

He cleared his throat. "Well, no."

"Why do I have to make good decisions all the time? I want to make a bad decision. I want to try something. I don't think it's up to you to decide whether or not I get to do something crazy. So, I'm off."

"Dammit, Honey."

"Damn *you*, Jericho." She walked past him, and then he grabbed her by the arm, whirling her to face him. She felt like all the breath had been sucked out of her body as she stared into his thunderous face.

She took stock of him. Of his beautiful features. His dark brown eyes and skin, the black stubble that covered his square jaw. And she felt like he was taking up all the space. In addition to having taken this winery from her, he had stolen her ability to breathe. Her ability to think. And right now it just enraged her.

"Let go of me."

She wouldn't allow him to steal this from her too. He had been her most secret, most shameful fantasy for far too long, and she was on her way to make something new, to get something new. She was going to have what she wanted. And she did want Donovan. Or at least, she really wanted to want Donovan. And that was going to have to be enough, because she couldn't have Jericho.

Ever.

He was now the emblem of everything ruinous.

And she had called her brothers out for being dumbasses more than once, too many times to ever let herself be a dumbass over a man.

You don't think that you're being dumb about Donovan?

No. She wasn't. Because the simple truth was… He was handsome, and maybe having a fling with him would be fun. But it wouldn't devastate her. There was no way that it could. Because the ranch wasn't the family winery.

And he wasn't a man that was so close to her brothers he was practically family.

And he didn't… He didn't make her itch under her skin.

He didn't get to places that she couldn't reach.

So there was no risk involved. Jericho represented too much risk. Every risk. Every risk she couldn't take.

So yes, she could run away to Lake Oswego. She could hook up with a guy who may or may not be permanent. But she could never… She could never.

She jerked away from him and climbed up into the cab of her truck, defiant. Then she slammed the heavy door and unrolled her window. "I'm leaving."

"Yeah, you're doing a real convincing job of it too."

"I'll run your ass over if you get in my way."

"Honey…"

"Look, Merry Christmas and whatever. And good luck with your family. I don't hate you." Her throat suddenly got tight. "I just can't be here."

She started the engine, and before she could think better of it, she put the truck in Drive and punched the gas. And then she was leaving. Driving away from the little house she had called her own for years. From the winery that had always been her home. From the man who had given her butterflies in her stomach since before she knew what it meant.

This was better. Because she couldn't stay here. Held back, held in place, not anymore. Everyone else had moved on. And she would have to watch Jericho bring an endless succession of women to the winery for sex for the rest of her life. And never resolve the feelings that she had… Never move on. She hated how much this was about that. How much it was about him.

So she drove away, and she challenged herself not to look back. She was not going to look back.

And pretty soon the road became less familiar, winding and lined with trees. And as she went up in elevation, what had started as a light dusting of the snow turned into big banks of it piled up on the sides of the road.

Luckily, it wasn't cold enough right now to turn anything to ice.

She was on her way. She was on her way. She had quite a few miles of the middle of nowhere before she hit the interstate, and so she plugged her new phone in and cranked some country music, singing along with Luke Bryan, but pretty soon the lyrics of the song made her too sad. And she couldn't even say why, because it was a party tune about someone being excited to hear her song playing on the radio. Maybe it was because it reminded her of warm nights at the winery and sitting around with her family. Sitting with Jericho. Making s'mores and dancing up on the tailgate.

But the problem was, somewhere deep in her soul, that it always felt a little bit electric because he was there. And she just couldn't...

Why are you really mad?

She didn't want to think about that. She did not want to think about why she was really upset. Why she really needed to leave. Because him buying the vineyard had shown her something. That he really didn't think about her. And that she thought about him far too much. Way more than a woman should think about a man who had never showed any interest in her at all.

The road wound along the river, and she took in the beautiful scene. The rapids rolling over big smooth rocks, pine trees lining the banks and even a bald eagle giving her a patriotic show as he went fishing in the water.

And you're moving to the city.

It was not the city. It was the outskirts of

the city, and she would be at an equine facility. Really, it was completely up her alley. It was great. It was going to be fine.

Better than fine. Better than fine.

She was really full of affirmations today.

Sadly, she did not feel all that affirmed.

Suddenly, her truck sputtered slightly and gave a jolt. She startled, looking around as if there would be answers for what the hell was going on out there in nature.

It sputtered again, and she pulled over to the side of the road, letting it idle as she started breathing hard.

It would be fine. It was fine.

She put it in Drive and started to maneuver back out onto the road, and it made a horrible grinding sound and then stopped.

Well. Shit.

She grabbed her phone to call her brothers and saw that she didn't have any bars.

What the hell? Had she driven back into 1996?

She got out of the truck and looked around.

It was freezing. The wind whipped up, the sky going gray.

It felt ominous.

She couldn't walk back to Gold Valley. She had driven more than an hour, and it would take her all day. On the route that she had driven, there was no town back or forward for at least fifteen miles.

This was…terrible.

Horrible.

No one knew where she'd gone, that she'd left, that she was coming…

Only Jericho knew and he wasn't expecting her to get in touch anytime soon. Donavan didn't even know to be expecting her.

Someone would happen down the road, she was certain of that.

She was not going to panic. There was no point panicking. She just had to deal. She had protein bars in the glove box. She reached over and opened it, grabbed one and opened it immediately, suddenly feeling ravenous. Because, of course, the prospect of being stuck here did not agree with her at all.

Someone would come by. It wasn't like she was in the middle of nowhere.

She tore open the bar and shoved the food into her mouth.

She was fine. It was fine. Forty-five minutes into sitting there, she felt much less fine. Especially when the first light snowflake tumbled from the sky.

Great. She was going to freeze to death on the side of the road. A frozen pathetic virgin, whose last thought wouldn't be the man she was going to have sex with, but her older brothers' best friend, whom she had left behind.

She laid her head back against the seat and groaned.

And instantly, her mind conjured up summer. Summer, and Jericho half naked at the ocean. Wearing nothing but a pair of swim shorts, low on his hips. She could still remember the way that line cut right there, lowering her IQ by several points. His washboard abs, his chest, with just the right amount of dark hair.

And his skin… She wanted to lick it. And she had never licked another person in her life, but she was absolutely confident she wanted to lick him.

And punch him. In fairly equal measure most of the time. And what the hell was that?

She pounded her head against the back of the seat now.

"And here you are, just beginning to be responsible and take control of yourself. Here is your reward."

Freezing in her truck.

She heard a truck engine before she saw one. She turned sharply, opening the driver's-side door and stumbling out of the cab of the truck quickly. She didn't even bother to put her coat and mittens on.

She just started to wave.

She was a motorist, and she was in distress. And she was going to make sure this person knew that she was distressed.

She hopped up and down, feeling ridiculous, but her desperation outweighed the ridiculousness by a fair amount.

It was a red truck, sort of a rusty red. And it did not take her long to realize…

No.

Of course.

The bane of her existence. The object of her desire.

That damn pain in the ass.

He turned his blinker on, and she took a step back, and then he pulled right into the outcropping where she had parked her truck.

"What the hell?"

She looked into Jericho's stormy face.

"Well," she said. "I am having some car trouble. And I have no cell service."

"Shit," he said.

"What are you doing?"

"I told you that I was leaving. I'm heading up north to go to this… Big Dalton family shindig. They rented some complex up in the mountains."

"Oh really?"

"In Washington."

"In Washington?"

"Yeah."

"Can you drop me off?"

"Drop you off?"

"We're repeating again. And yes," she said. "In Lake Oswego. That would be perfect. I could have a tow truck bring my truck up there. But then I don't have to delay anything."

She really badly needed to get there. She needed to see Donovan in person. She needed to get this all taken care of. She just really needed it.

"You want me to drive you up to your fancy equine facility booty call?"

"How many times have I watched you pick up squealing, giggling bridesmaids at bachelorette parties?"

It was a fair question. Because she had watched him. A lot. In fact, she had something of a running tally in her head. And she didn't like it. It made her want to vomit her guts out every time.

She hated the idea of a woman touching him. She hated it.

Some woman running her hands over those abs. The ones that she wanted to lick.

The ones that she hated herself for wanting to lick.

Because there was just no point to it. He was Creed and Jackson's best friend. He was basically a surrogate son to her father, and try as she might, she genuinely could not see Jericho as a brother. She just couldn't.

And he wasn't… He was never going to marry her.

She didn't want to marry him anyway. She wasn't even sure she wanted to get married. She didn't know what she wanted. She had been certain that it was the winery, but now that wasn't going to happen and she had to re-evaluate things. Wanting to lick somebody's abs did not equate to wanting to marry them.

But they couldn't just… They couldn't do anything. Not given the proximity of their lives. Not given just how enmeshed they were.

But that did not mean that she liked knowing that he was off fucking some other girl.

"It will be a few," he said.

"How many times have you watched me pick up a guy?"

She could practically hear him grinding his teeth together. "I haven't."

Her cheeks were hot, but she was determined to be bold in this. Her brothers had never been discreet about their sex lives, and Jericho certainly hadn't been. Why should she? "Drive me to my booty call," she said.

It was poetic in a way.

She would use Jericho as a vehicle to get rid of her virginity. Not… Just in the way that he was going to actually drive the vehicle that would lead her up to the guy that was going to take her virginity. And that would be perfect.

"Your brothers…"

"Can hardly expect that I don't have a sex life," she said, lying, since she clearly did not have a sex life, but she hoped that Jericho didn't know that.

"They probably aren't going to want to know about you having a sex life with some

guy who's going to be signing your pay-
checks."

"Right. Like you've never had an ill-advised
love affair."

He huffed a laugh. "I wouldn't call anything that I've ever had 'a love affair.'"

"We can stand around debating the seman-
tics of where you had your dick, Jericho, or
we can get out of the cold. I would like to get
out of the cold. Can you give me a damned
ride or not?"

She was incredibly proud of herself for not
falling apart completely for saying the word
dick in his presence, especially not when she
meant his actual dick, which made her feel
sweaty and hot and more than a little bit excited. She wasn't going to think about his
dick. No. She was not.

She really needed to take care of her virginity.

Not in the way she had been taking care of
it, which had been like a preservation proj-
ect. This was eradication.

"Yeah, I'll give you a ride."

"Brilliant," she said. She took a photo of exactly where the truck was and the mile marker it was by, grabbed her suitcase and hefted it out of the bed, slinging it over into Jericho's.

Then she climbed up into the passenger side.

Thankfully, the truck was warm. And she buckled up, snuggling into the much more comfortable seats.

"Your truck's fancy ass," she said.

"I'm rich as fuck," he said.

She raised her brows. "Must be nice."

"Didn't you get a bit of money from the sale?"

"Yeah," she said, idly adjusting the heater knob on the truck.

"So, why don't you buy yourself a new truck?"

"Well, I don't really want a new truck. I mean I don't really need one. I mean, I don't really know what I want. It'll take some trying to figure it out."

"Right. Hence the taking the new job with the guy that you're…"

"I like him," she said.

"Great," he said. "Happy for you."

"You don't seem happy for me."

"Did you want me to throw you a party? A 'Honey is going to get laid' party?"

"That's all you're thinking in terms of. Maybe I really like him."

"Sorry. But you don't seem like you do."

"You don't…" She sputtered. "You don't get to decide what I sound like."

They drove down the road, fat flakes building as they hit the windshield.

"Is this four-wheel drive?" she asked.

He shot her a sideways look. It clearly said: *What do you think?*

She continued, "I do like him."

"You have shown a lot more emotion over generally being pissed off with me than you have over being with him. Being horny for somebody is not the same as being into them. Like into them completely."

"Excuse me," she said. "I'm not horny for him. I am not a fourteen-year-old boy."

"If you're not horny, what's the point?"

"I oppose the terminology," she said.

"Oh, I'm sorry. Did you want to split hairs about your sex language?"

"I would rather not get into sex language with you. How about that?"

"Suit yourself."

She cleared her throat. "It doesn't bother you to use it with me?"

"Hell no. I say it to anybody. I'd say it to your brothers."

"So I am…the same as my brothers to you."

"Yeah," he said.

"Bullshit," she practically screamed, but she was losing her mind here. He was not one of her brothers. He was being a possessive, demanding jerk, and he wasn't even one of her brothers. But worse, he was a man she wanted to be possessive of for all the wrong reasons. Still wrong. Still not what she wanted. Never what she wanted.

"You would not want Jackson or Creed to

go sleep with somebody that they were working with. Hell, Jackson was working with Cricket when he started to have sex with her. She's my age. Also, Creed was working in opposition to Wren when he had unprotected sex with her in a wine cellar. He got her pregnant. They're ridiculous. They are so irresponsible with sex that even I know all about their sex lives, and I really shouldn't. I am their sister, and I oppose that I know so much about it. But because they've been such idiots, the entire town is aware of it. So the fact that you're trying to warn me off sleeping with somebody just because I'm going to work at his ranch proves definitively that you don't actually think of me the way that you do Jackson and Creed."

He looked at her for a moment, lifting a brow. "Who said I didn't tell them they were being dumbasses?"

"Did you?" she pressed.

"Not in so many words, no, but I didn't really want to get punched in the face."

She turned, balled her hand into a fist and

slugged his shoulder. He was so muscular his flesh didn't even budge. It was like punching a granite wall.

"You tool," she said, shaking her hand.

"Honestly, language. And you were upset about *horny.*"

"And fuck you," she said.

"All right, I don't think of you as your brothers," he said. The windshield wipers on his truck were moving faster now. Working overtime. Trying to keep up with the snowfall.

"You wouldn't want me to anyway."

"You don't get to say what I want," she said.

"You're awfully spiky," he said.

"I have a right to be spiky," she returned. "You're being patronizing."

"I'm not intending to be patronizing. But the fact of the matter is, you are younger than us. And I worry a little bit about you."

That last comment made her feel like she was on uneven ground. But her fury still lingered, even while his concern wound its way around her heart. "You worry about me so much that you took my livelihood out from under me without a second thought."

"I didn't the hell know you wanted the winery, Honey, and I'm not invested in you not having it. We should've talked about this before you went off half-cocked."

"I'm about to go get a whole cock, thank you very much."

"I'm sorry, but *horny* was offensive?"

She chewed the inside of her cheek, feeling red and embarrassed and mad. She was just so... It wasn't fair. None of it was fair.

"This weather is getting intense," she said.

"Yeah," he said.

But something about the way he said that made her think that he wasn't really thinking of the weather.

They ended up not talking for a while, and she fiddled with the radio until she eventually gave up and just plugged her phone into his cable, firing up her country playlist. But he didn't complain.

It transitioned from Luke Bryan to Mickey Guyton, and she tried to focus on the song lyrics and not on the fact that the cab of the truck suddenly felt too small.

But about fifteen minutes into their determined silence, making commentary on the weather wasn't just to deal with awkwardness. It actually really merited a comment.

"This is crazy," she said.

The snow was beginning to truly pile up on the side of the road and starting to actually cover the road in earnest.

"It's fine," he said.

"I'm glad that you have so much confidence in your truck. That seems just like a man."

"No, it's spoken like a woman whose truck gave out a few miles back in good weather. I have a decent vehicle. It's going to be fine."

But the snow escalated until they couldn't see in front of them. Jericho slowed his truck to a crawl, maneuvering over the road as best he could.

"Shit," he said. "I might have to pull off. I can't see a damn thing." Just then, a big truck hauling logs came by in the oncoming lane. They didn't see it until it was right on top of them. It breezed by them so close, hugging the yellow line and making Honey jump.

She put her hand on his forearm, breathing hard.

"Good Lord," she said.

"Yeah," he said. "I'm going to have to pull off till it eases up. Assuming I can find a spot. See a spot."

"Where the hell are we?"

"Somewhere between Gold Valley and Lake Oswego," he said.

She thought she should probably laugh at that comment, because obviously… But her heart was still beating too quickly.

He took his phone out, and she could see that he didn't have any bars. She didn't hold out any hope that it meant she would either. He pulled off slowly, and she could feel the truck slide, then sink.

"Oh…" she said. "We're not going to be able to get back out."

"We'll be able to get back out."

Not today.

Not soon.

He didn't say that but she knew it. So did he. The snow didn't ease.

They sat there, the engine idling, the heater doing its best to keep them from freezing.

"I thought I was going to die in my truck all alone. But it turns out I'm going to die in your truck sitting next to you. I have to tell you, it is not an infinitely more cheering prospect."

"We're not going to die," he said.

"You don't know that."

"No," he said. "I don't know that on any given day. But I don't figure as a matter of course that I'm going to die, and I don't really figure it now."

"But again," she said. "You don't know."

"For the love of God, Honey."

He didn't say anything after that. He was just breathing in irritation.

Hard and heavy, and she became very aware of her own breathing. Of her heart beating. She turned to look at him, suddenly afraid.

"What are we going to do?"

"Not panic," he said.

"This is how people die," she said.

"Yeah," he said. "It is. But I'm not going to let anything happen to you. You understand?"

His brown eyes were sincere, and that was so unusual that it twisted up her insides. Plus she was afraid.

And for some reason, it was stirring deep truths and longings inside her. Making her feel shaken.

She suddenly felt very aware of how close they were. Of the heat coming off his body. Especially as things outside began to cool.

"I'm not going to let anything happen to you," he said. He moved his hand across the empty space on the truck seat and placed it over hers. "I swear."

She shivered, looking away. "Okay."

"It's going to be all right."

"I believe you," she said.

She jerked her hand away, feeling suddenly beset by his touch.

It didn't mean anything to him. He was comforting her like he would a child. But it made her too hot. Even in all this cold. They both knew that no one was going to happen by. Because everybody was getting off the road. There was not going to be any help coming for them unless it was somebody specifically looking for people who were stuck.

And neither of them were relishing the prospect of sleeping outside, she was sure.

"I'm going to get out and take a look around."

"No," she said, leaping forward, grabbing onto his hand. "People do that and they don't come back."

"I'm going to come back."

"They always think they will."

"I will not get away from the view of the truck. I promise you."

"Promise," she said. "You know… You know that happened to that man… The family got stuck and he walked away and…"

"I know," he said. "But I'm not going to lose sight of the truck. I just need to see if there's anyone else around here. Or if there's a house even."

"This is the middle of nowhere."

"It's the middle of we don't know where. That's a fact. So I'm just going to see."

And then Jericho opened up his truck door and stepped out into the snow.

Three

The weather outside made a witch's tit look like Hawaii. It was cold. And he was not prepared for a blizzard. But then, he didn't figure there was going to be a blizzard. Sure, there had been a forecast for snow, but it was Oregon. The much talked about snow apocalypse was always only ever a few flakes. If anything, you might get a foot, but nothing like this. Nothing like this. This was unprecedented. And crazy.

He kept his word to Honey, keeping one eye on the truck as he walked up and down the side of the road, then took a step into the woods to see if he could see houses.

Under the cover of the trees there was less snowfall, and there was better visibility. That was good.

His hand burned. From where he had covered hers with his. Ill-advised. But she had been afraid. And he'd have been a bigger jerk if he hadn't tried to comfort her.

There was something about the fact she was telling him all this when she'd told no one else that made it feel different.

There was also something about being away from the vineyard, sitting with her in his truck, that made her feel different. It made things between them feel different, and he couldn't say that he liked it overly much.

It was just… Not what it was supposed to be.

Right, and you need to be thinking about this while you're in a survival situation?

He kept thinking of the way she'd said *dick*. *His* dick, in fact.

Honey used vulgar language all the time. It

was kind of her thing. She was surrounded by men, and he kind of assumed that she tended to overdo it a little bit to prove that she was one of them.

But that was different. It felt different.

He felt it right on the aforementioned body part.

Just find some shelter, asshole.

All right, so he'd lied to Honey a little bit. He took hold of his scarf, unwrapped it from his neck and set it right next to a tree that was parallel to the car. As long as he kept a visual on that, he would be fine. The visibility was just so much better in the woods.

He pushed forward, always keeping the scarlet red of that scarf in his view.

He was looking for a house. Someplace that would have a phone so that they could call.

Anybody out here would have a landline. Or a phone that managed to get service somehow.

And then he saw it, just barely visible under the cover of the trees. A cabin. It was huge, but there were no lights on. It didn't look like anyone was there.

Well. He was not sitting on the side of the road with Honey. And… Hell. If he had to break into the place to use a landline, he would.

He crossed the expansive trees and went up through the back of the house. He knocked just in case. But there was nothing. No one.

There was a lockbox on the door, like it was something that was for sale. He checked every window and found one in the back ajar. He pushed it up, popped the screen out and climbed in.

And he really the hell hoped that he didn't trip a burglar alarm, or anything of the kind, because he didn't especially want to get shot, either by a homeowner or a cop, in the pursuit of shelter. But this was an emergency. He laughed, because no cop was going to come out here even if a burglar alarm was tripped.

So there was that. The weather had caused the problem, but at least it was helping with this part.

He walked through toward the front door and saw a big basket sitting there. There were bottles of wine in it, and there was a piece of paper sitting in a plastic sleeve.

He looked down at it. Welcome to Pineview. There were instructions for everything in the house, plus a list of amenities.

A vacation rental. He'd stumbled on a vacation rental. Hell.

He went to flip on some lights, and realized there weren't any. Then he looked down at the paper again.

In this off-grid retreat...

Well. Shit. However, he could see from the amenities paper that there should be a way to start a fire. A way to get lights going. And there were generators. For the hot water and for the toilets. All in all, it could be worse.

The paper also had a code to access the lockbox, and he did so, taking the keys out with him, before going back and replacing the screen on the window and closing it.

Wine in hand, he walked out the front door and back toward where he left the scarf.

From there, he made his way to the truck.

The visibility was so poor. He could hardly see.

He jerked the door open on the passenger side of the truck, and Honey jumped. "Oh," she said. "I did not see you."

"This is ridiculous," he said, pulling the door open with great effort. The snow was up to the bottom of it, piling higher and higher.

"Come on out," he said.

She did, as best she could. But there was a fair amount of wrestling with the snow in trying to get the door to open.

"Crazy," she said.

"I know it."

They both had suitcases in the back that were now covered with snow.

"What exactly are we doing?"

"I found a house."

"And they're letting us come inside?"

"Kind of."

He hefted her suitcase out of the back of the truck and handed it to her. Then he took her free hand with his and led her into the woods.

She was wearing gloves, which offered a barrier to their touch. But he still felt the fact that he was holding Honey Cooper's hand.

She dropped hold of it when they were beneath the trees. He stopped and gathered his scarf.

"What was that?"

"A marker. I didn't keep the truck in sight. But I kept that in sight, and I knew that the truck was just parallel to it."

"Of course you couldn't just be safe," she said.

"Hey, I found a house," he said. "You should just be thankful."

"That's a very male thing to say," she said.

"I'm a man," he responded.

"Sure," she said.

He gestured in front of them. "It's just through here." They went through the trees, and the house was still there, standing dark.

"I thought you said…"

"I didn't say anything. It's a vacation rental."

"A vacation rental."

"Handily, with a list of amenities right inside."

He pushed open the door, and she followed behind him.

"Damn," she said. "It's as cold in here as it is out there."

"But dry," he said. "It's off-grid."

"Off-grid," she squeaked.

She looked so distressed it might have been funny if there was anything funny about it. "Yeah," he said. "But there's fire starter. And it's designed to be this way. So, if the power goes out in the broader world everywhere, we'll be just fine here."

"Because the power's already out," she said.

"But again," he said. "Set up for it." He gestured around. "Lanterns."

"Seems a fire hazard," she said.

"Are you going to get overly excited and knock any of the lanterns down?"

"No," she sniffed.

"Well then, I expect it's fine."

He watched as Honey wandered around the

room, setting her suitcase down and ferreting about.

He looked down at the paper. "So if we get the generators to fire up, you can use the bathrooms."

"Well, thank God for that. I wouldn't have relished going outside to take care of things."

"No," he said.

"What else have we got?"

"There's a store of food. A root cellar and some evaporative cooling. Apparently. The off-grid experience is enhanced by the foods that they stock and provide. There is salted meat."

She looked around as if everything in the room might be a potential threat. And damned if he didn't find it...cute.

What the hell. He didn't do cute.

"Well," she said. "I feel like a pioneer."

"You don't sound thrilled about it."

"In fourth grade we had to spend an entire year playing *Oregon Trail*. I had enough party members die of dysentery to be cured of this fantasy."

"I always liked *Oregon Trail*."

"Sure. As a game. Less so as something I actually have to experience. I do not have an endless supply of bullets with which to go hunt buffalo."

He leaned into the humor of the moment because it was that or lean into the tension, and he didn't want to do that. "You wouldn't be able to find any buffalo in this weather anyway."

"Maybe they have some of the salted meat," she said.

"I guess we'll have to find out."

"Right now I'm more cold than I am hungry. I stuffed a protein bar in my face before you came to pick me up."

"Why?"

"I felt imperiled. Which made me feel hungry."

"Right. Well. Fair enough."

She scampered into the living room and he followed behind her. And saw that she was already taking out the fire starting gear from the basket near the hearth.

"Looks pretty good."

In this room there was a large fireplace. And he had noticed that there was a den off to the side where there was a woodstove.

That would actually likely produce more effective heat.

He assumed that whatever they cooked on in the kitchen also ran on wood heat. And it might benefit them to fire everything up.

"You got this?"

"Of course I've got this," she said. "I'm a country girl."

He chuckled. It was getting dark outside, and he took one of the lighters and a little lantern and decided to carry it with him.

The cabin was cavernous, massive, but it was also solid and sturdy and fairly well insulated from the cold outside. Rustic, but comfortable.

The furniture was expensive, very nice. There was a big bedroom with a large king-size bed. And furs covering what looked like a pretty plush mattress.

And instantly, he pictured laying Honey down on those furs.

The image was so stark, so clear, that it made him jerk back. Shit. He could not be having thoughts like that. That just wasn't going to fly.

There was a big fireplace in there, which was good.

The other two bedrooms did not have a heat source.

He assumed that this place was mostly for rent during the summer. He couldn't imagine people going to the trouble of trying to rent it this time of year. And with weather like this it was basically a liability. He went back down the stairs, and there was a raging fire going in the living room.

"Well done," he said.

"I'm not entirely useless," she said.

"You're not even a little bit useless. I'm pretty damn sure you know that." Their eyes met and held for a long moment.

And it made him conscious of how alone they were.

And how beautiful she was.

He looked away.

"I don't know. Sometimes I feel a little bit like I might be useless."

"Is this about the winery again?"

"It's hard for things not to be about the winery right now."

"I get that. I really do. I get it. But I don't think it was actually a commentary on you. Your dad wanted out from under it. He told me…he hasn't really been happy there for a long time. You may not believe this, but he approached me about it. I'm not sure that he's thinking any deeper than that. He's not capable of seeing the winery as a dream right now."

"Well, but…"

"He cautioned me plenty, even as he offered it. But the thing is, it's in a much different state now than it was all those years ago when he first started. It's profitable, it's got a full staff. Asking Jackson to look after things is kind of a formality. I think your dad sees a younger person wanting to take over the winery and remembers himself at my age…"

Honey snickered.

"What's so funny?" he asked.

"A younger person."

"I'm young," he said.

This was just insulting. He was in his midthirties, for heaven's sake, and this child, who was not a child at all, but a woman he found incredibly attractive, was laughing at him.

"Not really."

"Wow."

"Well. I'm just saying. You're not as young as I am."

Damned if he didn't know that.

"No," he said. "I'm not."

"Just making sure you remember."

Suddenly, that statement took on an edge, and it sliced through his gut like a knife.

"All right," he said. "Quit mouthing off and let's figure out something to eat."

"I hope that nobody's going to show up," she said.

"I don't think anyone's showing up. Even if they had a reservation… If we can't get out, people sure can't get in."

"Fair. This is so wild."

She stood and looked out the window, and he gazed at her, silhouetted by the waning light. The snow was beginning to pile up in earnest, even with the cover of the trees.

"There's no internet. Obviously. And there's no service. So until we are able to get out of here… We're not going to be able to get in touch with anyone."

"Great. So my truck is just going to be sitting up where we left it. Good thing I brought my stuff."

"Good thing."

"What are the Daltons going to think when you don't show up?"

He laughed. Hard and without humor. "Probably that I had second thoughts. About joining that circus."

"Well, I guess that would be fair."

"Yeah. Definitely."

"You never seem to be really affected by

anything, and I guess I didn't really appreciate how weird it must be to find out you have this whole big family."

"I've known," he said.

"Oh," she said. "Well, I guess it must be weird to get an invitation to join it then."

"It's all weird. But… On the scale of things I've been through in my life, it doesn't really register. I felt like why not go." But even to his own ears that sounded hollow. If he didn't care, he wouldn't be going. But the truth of the matter was, he wasn't entirely certain why he was going. He just didn't have a good answer. Not for himself. Not at all. He didn't know what he wanted to prove, though he would like to think that he wanted to prove nothing. That he literally didn't care at all about Hank Dalton or what he thought. That he didn't have any desire to get to know his half siblings.

But there were a lot of them. And nieces and nephews too. And… Yeah, all right. Once you had an invitation to join in with the big family, it just seemed… He just wanted to see. He wanted to see what they were like. He wanted to see if he was like them.

Hardheaded and stubborn and determined.

He knew that Hank and Tammy Dalton were white trash from way back, and then Hank had done good in the rodeo and gotten a lot of money. That the money had managed to buy them class.

He knew they were hardscrabble and determined people, whose fights had always been legendary in town.

Jericho himself had a hot temper, he was more determined than most and he had been certain that he was meant for better things than what he was born to. And he had done all that he could to make that possible. He'd worked with his hands and used his brain to figure out the best usage of his work ethic. Basically, he had to wonder if he got some of that from Hank.

Granted, he knew he got plenty of spirit from his mom, who had been a beautiful woman, and a fighter. All the way to the end.

"Sorry," she said.

"No need to apologize. It's a weird situation. But it is what it is."

"You know," Honey said, wrinkling her nose. "For a while there, Cricket thought that she might be our half sister."

Jericho sputtered. "Really?"

"Yeah. She's not."

"Yeah, judging by the fact that she is now engaged to your brother, and they're having a baby, I figured."

Honey shrugged. "Well. It's just… Families are complicated. Is my point."

"Yeah. I know. Though I've always been kind of short on family."

She looked away. "You've always been like family to us."

He arched a brow. "Right. You just love me."

"Well, when you're not being annoying."

"Why don't you make yourself useful and start a fire in the woodstove. I'll go dig around for food?"

And then Honey left him sitting there, pondering the moment. And pondering the strange interruption to his life that this was. He been on his way to deal with this family stuff, and now he was here.

With her.

Far too much temptation for him to consider.

He didn't know what the hell any of it meant. And he had to wonder if by the end of it he would have a better idea, or if it would just be one of those things.

Not everything in life means something. Sometimes it's just a shitty detour.

Yeah. Well. He just hoped the shitty detour had decent food.

Four

Honey managed to find the root cellar, and in it the evaporative coolers. There were vegetables in there, remarkably well-preserved. Which only reinforced her theory that the house had been intended to receive visitors.

She hummed as she dug around for food, trying not to overthink the moment that had happened in the living room.

She really hadn't given a lot of thought to this whole situation with Jericho and the Daltons.

But then, she didn't know what to make of

it. And they didn't exactly confide in each other. Mostly they just...bickered.

Because he made her feel strange, and if she wasn't saying something, they were sitting in silence, and she didn't like sitting in silence with him.

She found bacon and eggs, and some potatoes, and decided to go with breakfast for dinner. Unfortunately there was no pop can of biscuits, which would've made everything complete, and she wasn't about to go scrounging around for baking supplies.

There was a basket sitting by the door of the root cellar, and she grabbed hold of it, put her spoils inside and walked back up the stairs to the main level of the house.

The whole place was beautiful. High-gloss logs that built a sturdy, impressive-looking house. She just couldn't understand why anybody would choose to put a house this beautiful right out in the middle of nowhere with no amenities. Though, she supposed these were amenities. They were just a lot more work than the amenities she was used to.

She walked into the kitchen, and he was standing there, stripped down to a T-shirt, stoking the fire underneath the woodstove. His brown skin gleamed in the light, his muscles shifting with each movement.

He took her breath away.

And that was silly. She really needed to get a hold of herself.

"Breakfast for dinner," she said, lifting the basket.

"Perfect," he said.

"I did find ketchup."

"Well, that is the important thing."

"Absolutely. You can't have eggs or hash browns without a whole bunch of ketchup."

"On that we agree."

"Well, glad to know there's something. Maybe the secret to world peace is ketchup."

"Somehow I doubt it."

"What would it be then?"

He frowned. "Ranch dressing?"

"They don't have ranch dressing everywhere."

"All the more reason to use it as an agent

of world change. People just need to know about ranch dressing," he said.

"Also true."

His dark brows shot up. "Two agreements in under a minute. We may survive this."

"Yeah, and I have bacon in this basket. So..." He chuckled. He straightened and crossed his forearms over his broad chest.

Her heart thundered.

"I turned on the generator. For the bathroom. So, all that's functional. And if you want to shower..."

"Oh," she said, suddenly feeling a little bit fluttery. "Thank you. That's great."

"As far as I can tell, it's got enough gasoline to run for a bit. But we probably don't want to run it constantly."

"The appeal of off-grid living escapes me," she said.

"I have to say, I like a modern amenity."

"Careful, I'm going to start thinking we're friends."

"Oh, God forbid."

She forced a smile, then started to root

around through the cabinets, producing a frying pan, some cooking oil and the cheese grater. She found a potato peeler and stuck it in Jericho's hand. "Care to make yourself useful?"

"Amend that," he said. "I have been very useful this entire time."

She rolled her eyes. "Oh certainly," she said.

He moved alongside of her, grabbing the potatoes and starting to peel them into the trash. His muscular forearms flexed and shifted, and she did her best not to be distracted by it. And she did her best to ignore it while she sliced the bacon off the slab—which she had never done before—and cracked the eggs into a bowl, whisking them around.

It was a little bit of a learning curve, figuring out how to get everything onto the stove without burning it or causing huge drama, but owing to the basic nature of the meal, she managed to put together something nice. The dishes were camp plates. Blue tin with white speckles, and she found herself overwhelmed by nostalgia holding on to them. She couldn't even quite say why.

Until an image came into her head of her mother sitting at the table in the kitchen, holding a mug made of the same material. She smiled. "My mom used to like this kind of thing."

"Living off-grid?"

"No, these camp dishes." Her heart squeezed, and the image in her head got fuzzy around the edges. "My memories of her are so thin. I wish there were more. I wish I'd understood I was losing her so I would have held on to every memory more than I did."

"I'm sorry. From what I remember of her, she was great," he said. "I... I was glad I got to know her even if it was for a short amount of time."

She cleared her throat. "Yeah. I'm glad too. She really loved you, you know."

"That's how I met your brothers, you know."

"How?"

"Because both of our moms were sick. That sucked. And of course at school... That was something people talked about. Then I lost my mom. I related to what they were going through with your mom's illness… It's not a great thing to be bonded over, that's for sure. Because it just kind of sucks."

"Yeah," she said. "It does."

"But your dad… He found out about my living situation, and he took me in. I don't know if you realize just how much I depended on your family."

She frowned. "No. I didn't. I didn't think about it. It was just that one day you didn't really leave."

"Well, if not for your dad, I was either going to have to figure out becoming an emancipated minor or possibly going into the system. And I didn't really relish that. He became my legal guardian… He made sure that I had everything I wanted. He did what Hank Dalton never did. He was like a father to me."

"Jericho…" Guilt twisted her. Because she hadn't realized all this. She'd been a kid, and she'd been consumed with the changes in her own family, and of course consumed with the fact that she thought he was handsome. And the associated torture therein.

She had never really thought about his losses. About the strangeness of his relationship to Hank Dalton. About...

You've never thought about him as a person. He's been an object. There to be good-looking to you, irritating to you...

Yeah. Well, turns out he wasn't exactly the crappiest person in their relationship. It was her. It left her feeling rocked. Because she had spent so much time absolutely certain no one understood her. But how much of an effort had she ever made to really understand the people around her?

She was sure she was stoic because they all simply were.

Were they also trying to protect her? Protect themselves?

"I'm sorry that I never thought about that," she whispered, the words coming out raspy. "It's pretty much inexcusable."

"It's fine, Honey."

Her chest felt sore, and her heart was beating hard. She didn't like it. "No. I've been a brat to you. Always."

He stared at her, long and hard. "You know I never forgot. That you are just a little girl who lost her mom the way that I did. I didn't forget. Because I'm older than you. Because I got to have some perspective along with my grief. You were a kid. And…"

"I'm not a kid now. And it seems that I haven't done a very good job of recognizing…the full picture of things."

"I think that's pretty normal."

"Stop absolving me for being a jerk. I don't deserve it."

"Since when is any of this about what we deserve."

"I don't know. I just know that… I should've been a better friend."

"You're a pretty good friend. You made some bacon."

"Yeah, well you saved my life. What if you hadn't of happened by? I would be completely stuck in my truck in this blizzard. Nowhere to go. No cell service, no hope of rescue.

Because at a certain point people that were smarter than us got off the road."

"Well, I did happen by. And here we are."

She looked around. "Yeah. Here we are."

"I guess there's not really much to do up here."

"There's some bookshelves."

"Yeah, I noticed that. Maybe I'll finally get around to reading *Lord of the Rings*."

She wrinkled her nose. "I think I'll stick with the field guide of birds that I saw earlier."

"Birds, huh?"

Why couldn't he just let her find a thing to do to distract herself so they didn't have to talk?

She sniffed. "I like birds, Jericho."

"Like *particularly*, or in comparison to how much you like hobbits?"

She huffed a laugh. "No. *I like birds*."

"What's to like about birds?"

"They're…cute. Or majestic. Or *menacing*. Birds can be all three. I admire it." Then she added, "I aspire to it."

"They're also good fried," he said.

She scowled. "Yes. But that isn't… I'm not reading a recipe book. I am reading a *field guide*."

"Well, enjoy your field guide."

"Perhaps I will."

They finished eating, and she gave thanks for the running water, rinsing off all the plates while Jericho dried and put them away. Then they retreated to the living room, where they had built a big fire, and she pretended to peruse the illustrated guide to birds while he did a good impression of somebody reading a thick fantasy novel.

And really, she was just suddenly overwhelmed. By the isolation. By his proximity.

By the fact that she had intended to be with another man tonight. Losing her virginity.

And suddenly the idea made her feel strung out. On edge.

Suddenly it made her feel… Way too much of everything. She also thought of her suitcase, which was currently full of lingerie.

And she swallowed hard.

She turned her focus to the Mott Mott. Which was an interesting enough bird. But not half as interesting as the intrusive thoughts swirling around in her head. Which should not be interesting, but problematic. Very, very problematic.

"Well," she said. "I'm sleepy."

"It's probably about that time," he said.

"We'll let the fire die out."

"Oh."

"I started one upstairs a bit ago."

"Oh good."

Except her throat was dry, and it didn't particularly feel good. It felt…like something, and it shouldn't feel like something. They were just out here surviving together. There was nothing happening. No undertone to the offer of preparing beds and fireplaces.

She followed him upstairs, and it took a moment for things to begin to dawn on her fully.

"Wait… You started one?"

"The other bedrooms don't have fireplaces,"

he said. "If you want to stay warm… This is the room."

He pushed the door open and revealed a master bedroom, with a roaring fire and a massive bed covered in blankets and furs.

"Oh but…"

"It's not a big deal," he said. "It's a huge bed."

"But…"

"Is it a problem?"

A thousand thoughts cascaded through her head. Yes, it was a problem. She had never shared a bed with a man in her life, and now she was supposed to sleep next to the most beautiful man she'd ever known. Now she was supposed to… What the hell? How was she going to survive this? How was she going to survive this?

"You seem bothered," he said.

She did her best not to sputter outrageously. "I am *unbothered*."

"I brought your suitcase up too. If you want to get in some pajamas."

She thought about the pajamas she had

brought. All of a rather lacy nature. Because she had been planning on…

She swallowed hard.

"You know. I think I'm just going to sleep in this. For warmth."

"Suit yourself."

"Do you need to… You need to change into…pajamas?"

He fixed her with a hard stare, his dark eyebrows lifted. "No. I think I'll stick with this."

"It's okay…"

"I don't wear pajamas, Honey."

"You don't…"

He slept naked.

The truth slammed into her hard. And she felt it between her legs. Oh gosh. She was failing at not making this sexual. This thing that would never be sexual to him because of course he didn't feel that way about her at all.

"Well, then." She coughed. "Stay in your jeans."

"Somehow I thought that might be your stance."

She decided she just better rip the Band-Aid

off. She got into the bed quickly, lifting at the edge of one of the furs and sliding beneath it, huddling on one edge of the bed.

It was so warm. It was luxurious. There had been a slight chill to everything, and the quilt, combined with the furs, took the edge off.

She was far enough on one side of the king-size bed that she didn't even feel it when Jericho got in.

She gave thanks for that. If she stayed on her edge, she should be all right.

She closed her eyes and tried to make her breathing sound normal. Tried not to sound like somebody who was faking being asleep.

"I'll tend the fire."

She opened one eye. "You don't have to do that by yourself."

"It's no big deal."

"But it's not... I mean..."

"Honey, don't worry about it. Get some sleep. If this turns into a multiday thing, then we may have to have conversations about who's manning the fire and who's not. But right now… We don't need to make a big deal out of it."

"Oh. Okay."

"Get some sleep. Because tomorrow is going to be a full-time job to keep ourselves warm. And fed."

"Hopefully the snow will have stopped by then." How long could it possibly do this? It had to stop. Tomorrow it would warm up and things would melt.

It had to.

"Hopefully. But I don't have any way to check the forecast. So I've a feeling we'll be walking down to check the road intermittently."

"Yeah." She sighed. "You know, nobody's even going to realize that we are missing except for the Daltons. And since they're just going to think that you blew them off…"

"I know. Thankfully your truck is sitting there closer to town than mine. So, it's possible that somebody will realize."

She blinked. "Right."

But neither of them said what they were

both thinking, which was that they might be stuck here for a pretty long time. And that if they were, there wasn't going to be a whole hell of a lot that they could do about it.

They were just going to have to be very comfortable with each other.

And on that note, she curled up as close to the edge of the mattress as she possibly could. And closed her eyes tight.

Five

Jericho woke up and realized that the room was cold. And that he was *very* warm.

She wasn't touching him, but there was only a scant foot between the two of them, and he could feel the heat radiating off her body. He had tried initially to get under only one layer of the blankets, but it had just gotten so damned cold, that he had ended up surrendering to the need to get beneath them. And that put them far too close for his comfort.

And he needed to get that fire going again.

He stood up and looked out the window,

pulling the curtains back. It was gray, early. The sun would probably be up in another half hour or so. But he wasn't quite ready to face the day. Not considering what they had ahead of them.

Because the snow had piled up impossibly high underneath the trees, and one thing was certain, even if the snowplow had been out this far, his truck was stuck on the side of the road. And he was going to have to get to a space where he could get a tow truck.

And right now, none of that was looking likely.

So he got the fire going again, and eyed the bed. And the space Honey had crowded into.

He lay back down, one layer beneath the blankets, and stared directly up at the ceiling, trying to ignore the way her breath fanned over his neck.

She was Jackson and Creed's little sister. She was practically a sister to him. And what he'd said to her last night had been true. He had always known that she was just a kid grieving her mom.

And it had never really bothered him that she didn't treat him like there was something grieving and broken in him. It was funny to see her distress over it. Like she thought she should've been sweeter and kinder for some damned reason.

As if he was suddenly breakable, because she realized they shared a common grief.

He'd always known that.

The fact that she was such a determined person. The kind of person who did just sort of get along with things… That was one reason he… Well, he recognized it. Because life was hard, and somehow you had to keep going. She was good at that. And he admired it.

Gradually, he realized that he wasn't going to be getting back to sleep. And he decided the better part of virtue would be getting the downstairs warmed up and figuring out some breakfast. And most especially coffee. He figured round two of bacon and eggs wasn't the worst thing in the world, and did that up quickly, and then gave up a prayer of thanks when he found a percolator and some coffee.

He set that on to steep and then decided to go back to the bedroom.

He didn't grab a lantern because the light was gray, and he could see more or less, and he'd taken decent note of the layout of the place the night before.

He pushed the bedroom door open and saw Honey, now curled up firmly in the middle of the bed.

He started to cross the space, but bumped against the dresser and knocked her suitcase down. It popped open, landing on its end, the contents spilling out.

"Shit," he muttered, bending down to pick it up. He reached down to begin to shove the items back inside and recognized the texture of the handful of things that he grabbed.

Lace.

He had an entire handful of lingerie. Because the suitcase was… Well, hell, it appeared to be 90 percent see-through underwear.

He was frozen. Completely and totally frozen, and grateful for the fact that he couldn't see all that well, because if he had too much of a sense of the kind of panties Honey was into, he might just die of a heart attack. And he didn't need that kind of drama, not on everything else.

He didn't have that kind of restraint; he damn well did not.

But it was too late. Because he was already figuring out exactly what these panties consisted of from just a casual touch, and his mind was constructing highly visual fantasies.

He heard a squeaking sound, and then she sat up, just in time to see him crouched there, holding on to her clothes.

"What the hell are you doing?"

"I knocked your shit over," he said. And he shoved it back into the suitcase as quickly as possible and turned the thing flat.

"Don't go through my things," she said, climbing out of the bed and scrambling over to the suitcase, viciously pushing the clips back down.

"Sorry," he said. "I didn't mean to. I just

came to tell you that I made coffee. And bacon and eggs."

"Well, fine," she said.

"I'd suggest you get changed, but I don't think you have a change of clothes in there."

"Oh, you had to say something."

"Yeah. Apparently I did." He had meant to say something, because at the end of the day, it was his bad that he knocked the suitcase over and it wasn't really his business what was in it. But he had seen it. He couldn't unsee it. Not even a little bit.

"A gentleman wouldn't comment."

"I never said that I was a gentleman."

"Well, that is… That is very clear and obviously true."

"Settle down, Honey."

"Do not tell me to settle down. Do not tell me to settle down when you're the person who…who has been manhandling my things."

"Were you planning on actually working up there?"

"I was going to have the rest of my things

sent. But in point of fact, I was intent on launching a seduction."

"Hell. I need coffee."

He turned and stomped out of the room, went down the stairs.

And he heard her furious footsteps behind him.

"Not that it's any of your business," she said. "I was on a mission to lose my virginity."

Everything in him went quiet. Still.

He turned, and he couldn't really make out her face in the dim light. Couldn't tell if she was angry or horrified that she let that slip. Couldn't tell what she'd been thinking by doing it.

Virginity.

She had been going up there to lose her virginity to…

To some random dude.

And he would never, ever, be able to get that image out of his head. That Honey Cooper was a virgin.

That she was ready to lose it. That she had

a whole bunch of lingerie designed for that very thing in that suitcase up there.

He was only a man. And what really worried him was that he might have more in common with Hank Dalton than he had previously realized. Because he was a little bit of a womanizer and always had been, but this was something else. This felt like a compulsion. A tug.

And he didn't want to think about it. But it was there. And it was driving him.

And he felt…

It was deeper than the attraction he'd felt before.

Something in him felt like he would never really be satisfied if he didn't strip her naked right then and there, kiss her lips and…

Coffee.

"I am getting coffee," he said.

"Does that bother you? Does it bother you to know that I was taking control of my life and my sexuality?"

"I was happy to previously have never

thought about your sexuality," he said through gritted teeth.

Such a damned lie.

But a virgin? A virgin. He had not considered that. Not ever.

"Well. How nice for me. That's the problem, Jericho. I could stay in Gold Valley and remain a sexless, boring object that just sits around the winery, not seen as somebody who could take over, not seen as somebody capable of being the boss, not seen as an actual woman, or I could go off and make a life for myself.

"So maybe you don't understand why I might want to get a new job, or sleep with the man who gave me that job. Honestly, those things are accidentally linked. I met him on a dating site. I wasn't going to take work from him, but the offer came up. And it…it seemed infinitely better to what I had. Seemed infinitely better than dying on the vine out in Gold Valley."

"Let me tell you something," he said, breaking his own rule and mandate about going to get the coffee. "There's a whole lot out there in this world, good sex and bad sex, and none of it makes you who you are. You make you who you are, and there should be no reason to go out and fling your virginity at the nearest person you can find just because you're unsatisfied with the state of things."

"It doesn't matter, and yet you are lecturing me on the fact that I shouldn't throw my virginity away? Can you see how those two things conflict with each other?"

"Dammit," he said. "That's not the point of anything. Just sit… You don't need to find the first guy you're remotely interested in and…"

He didn't like any scenario, but for some reason he extra hated Donavan.

"You don't know who I'm interested in. You don't know who I have been interested in. And who I haven't been. You don't know as much about me as you think. Look, I admitted that I don't know as much about you as I should. That I kind of just saw you as… It doesn't matter. But the fact that you knew that I was a grieving little girl doesn't mean that you know me now."

"No. It doesn't. And if I'm honest… I figured that you… I mean… You're twenty-two."

"I know how old I am," she said.

"I figured you had." He gritted his teeth. "You know. If pressed to think about it."

"Well, I know you have, because you flaunted all over the place. And that's what I don't understand. How is it okay for you to do that, but you're all up in arms about me."

"I don't want you to get hurt," he said.

"Why do you think I would get hurt?"

"Because women *do*," he said. "They end up making rash choices about sex and they get hurt."

"Wow. That is the most… You are infuriating. And you have no right to comment on anything. None at all. I didn't want you to see that suitcase, I didn't want you to know about any of this."

"Why did you tell me?"

She sputtered. "I need coffee."

She brushed past him and went into the kitchen, grabbing hold of the percolator and the camp mug—that was identical to the plate she'd used last night—and pouring an amount in. "I guess it would be too much to hope that they had half-and-half."

"Sorry. Nothing quite so civilized."

"Well, that's just terrible."

She just served herself up a heaping portion of eggs and bacon, then retreated into the living room, where there was a fire going. He stayed in the kitchen, stood while he ate.

This was fine. It was early, and the situation they were in was weird. They didn't need to carry on talking about her hymen, or whatever. He didn't care about things like that. He never had.

So why his brain should be stuck on Honey and her sexual status, he didn't know.

Maybe because he'd been too damned fascinated by her to begin with, and now that he knew for a fact no man had ever touched her...

The idea of being the first one to do it...

Hell.

And no.

As if she hadn't been off-limits to begin with.

After he got the coffee into him, he felt a little more balanced. And he took himself into the living room, where Honey was sitting, her giant bird book on her lap, her empty plate beside her. She was studying the birds.

"How are the birds?"

"Much the same as I left them," she said, sniffing.

"Good. Good." He looked at her. "You know speaking of birds. And bees…"

"No," she said, holding up her hand. "I could happily never have this discussion with you, Jericho."

"Why not?"

"Because it's awkward. Because I'm going to die of being awkward."

"It's just…" He didn't know why he couldn't leave this alone.

He had to…deal with it. Talk about it until he wasn't so preoccupied with it. Make it feel like something normal and not taboo and definitely not the source of a host of new fantasies surrounding a woman he never should have had any fantasies about in the first place.

Let alone fantasies about being her first.

"Look," he said. "It's just that… Women get a lot of feelings around sex."

"Oh," she said. "*Women*. Women get a lot of feelings around sex. Which is why you are prowling around like an angry cat unable to drop the subject."

"I'm not prowling. Most especially not like a cat."

"Panther."

"Not less offensive."

"Why?"

He knew why. Because he felt like a predator all of a sudden. Stuck in the house with her. Like a fox in the henhouse, if he had to choose. No. He had control over himself. He was not Hank Dalton.

He looked at Honey, who was staring yet more resolutely at the birds.

"Are there new birds?"

She didn't look up. "I can report that there are no new birds since yesterday."

"But you seem very committed to the book."

"Just let me deal with the awkward situation by pretending to be engrossed. I think we both know that's what I'm doing. Why can't you do the same?"

He didn't know.

"Because. Ignoring stuff doesn't make it go away."

And that was the biggest load of bullshit he ever spewed in his life, because if he was good at one thing, it was ignoring feelings until they went away. Because he had been a lonely, sad kid who had just pushed those feelings aside and made himself tough. Because he had been forced to be grown before he ever should've been, taking care of his mother and missing so very much being the one that was taken care of. Because he had developed resentment heaped upon resentment at the father who wasn't there.

Who hadn't given them enough money to

survive the medical bills that were piling up. Because his mother—because of her pride—refused to accept any money from Hank, or to allow Jericho to ask for any. Yeah. He was a champion at ignoring emotions. A damned *king*.

And he flashed back to the moment in the winery before he found out that Honey was leaving. Before she yelled at him. And he suddenly had an inkling as to what was going on here. It was an excuse. An excuse that his body was latching onto like a champion. She had introduced something interesting, and he had taken that as an opportunity to swing wide the door on the attraction that had been building there for longer than he cared to admit.

It was harder right now to deny how attracted to her he was than it ever had been. His blood felt hot with it.

It had become harder and harder to think of her as the little girl she'd once been.

The image of her now had fully replaced the one of the past, and it was even hard for him to think of her solely as Jackson and Creed's little sister. They worked together. They spent a lot of time at the winery together. And he saw her, her moods, her work ethic. Her strength. She was snappy and feisty and every inch the kind of woman he'd love to tangle with if she weren't...

No. That was a lie. She was not the kind of woman he'd want to tangle with if she weren't Honey Cooper. Because she was too... She was too earnest. Everything that she felt and did came from a very real place. Including all the anger she'd spewed at him back at Cowboy Wines, and...even her running up north to go sleep with some guy. Because she was put out about the situation at the winery.

Like she was trying to shed her skin, shed her expectations. And he didn't do earnest. He didn't, because there was nothing he could do in the face of it. Because he had spent so many years deadening his own feelings. And he didn't know what to do with the person who simply...hadn't.

"Isn't there something to do? Like some

manly homesteading thing? That will get you out of my grill."

"I made you breakfast," he pointed out.

"And it was appreciated. The coffee was good. But… Isn't it a full-time job survival-ing?"

"*Survivaling* isn't a word."

"It is. It's what we're doing. We are surviv-aling."

"We're *surviving*."

"No. Because it's like—" she waved a hand "—survivalist stuff. It's not just like surviv-ing."

He huffed out a laugh. "Has anyone ever told you that you're ridiculous?"

But the ridiculousness didn't ease the tension. She was too cute, sitting there on the overstuffed couch by the fire, woolly socks on her feet, her brown hair in a loose knot on her head. As she held a giant book that opened across her whole lap and pretended to read it.

She looked up at him. "Oh. All the time."

"So, you want me to go survivaling. And

what are you going to do? Sit here reading about birds? How is that useful?"

"A solid database of avian knowledge can always be useful, Jericho."

He stared at her for a long moment. At the way the sun glowed on her skin. The curve of her cheekbones, her round, pink mouth. Her whiskey-colored eyes.

She was a pretty creature. No doubt about that.

The kind of pretty, delicate thing his hands could easily spoil. And he would do well to remember that.

"For what?"

"For example, I will know which birds we can cook and eat if it comes down to it."

"You know, I think I'm going to go ahead and hope we skip that part. There's no way the weather's going to keep up like this."

"I wouldn't have thought it would have kept up overnight," she said, putting the book down and scrambling to the window, looking outside. "I've never seen anything like this."

He didn't want to say that he hadn't either.

Didn't want to acknowledge that this was outside of his scope of experience. "It'll be fine. We are really very okay with our setup."

"Yeah. Except for the whole being out of touch with civilization."

"We don't need civilization. We have each other." He paused for a moment. "And bacon."

"The bacon won't last forever." Her voice sounded thin and it made his gut tighten.

They were talking about bacon.

"No." And he was a little afraid of what might happen if the two of them kept on in close quarters. But no, there was no reason to be afraid. He was in control of himself. In control of his body. Brief flashes of attraction, and a newfound fascination with her sexual status did not get to dictate what he did next.

And what he would do, was go chop wood.

Because that was useful. And it was not sitting here ruminating on things that he shouldn't.

"I'm going to go chop some wood. Best make me some bread."

"Bread?"

"Yeah, that's your women's work. For the survivaling."

That earned him her anger and damned it if didn't ignite a fire in his blood. He needed to go jump in a snowbank.

Good thing there were so many handy.

"*Really,*" she said.

"Well, once I'm done chopping wood I'm going to have expended a lot of calories."

"All right," she said. "I'll make you something. I can't promise it'll be bread. I don't have... Anything. And I'm not good at that stuff anyway. I know just enough to keep myself fed."

"Well, maybe it's your chance to expand your skills."

That hit. And it hit hard. And in spite of himself, he caught himself holding her gaze. Lingering.

It hit him deeper than it should.

Made him think of all kinds of skills he could help her expand.

His hands on her skin. Her body against

his. He'd denied it for so long now it was second nature. Wanting what he couldn't have was his natural state.

As a boy he'd wanted a father. He hadn't had one.

He'd wanted his mother to be well. He'd wanted to not be a caregiver, and he hadn't gotten that either.

Wanting Honey was just a piece of all that same longing he'd lived with his whole life.

No.

"Wood," he bit out.

And then he strode out, like the fire had leaped out of the fireplace and was chasing at his heels.

Six

Honey felt prickly and perturbed. As she had, ever since this morning's explosion with Jericho. She had not meant to tell him about her virginity. But then, he shouldn't have looked at all of her lingerie.

Still, the lingerie had not necessitated her confession. She didn't really know why she'd done it.

Maybe wanted to see what he'd do…

That made her breath quicken.

It was a strange thing, being trapped here with him. It was a lot like being in the den with a lion. And the problem with that was, she kept getting tempted to…feed herself to him.

The problem was, in close proximity like this it was difficult for her to forget that she was attracted to him. Wildly. But what had started as a fluttery sort of teenage feeling had lately become extremely adult and quite *imagination after dark*.

But she…

The fact was, she wanted him, and Donovan had only ever been a surrogate for that. Because she felt like her attraction to Jericho was emblematic of the fact that she had held on to her virginity for too long. But she had convinced herself that she could rid herself of her issues by just losing it to anybody. And now she was beginning to wonder.

It was a really distressing thing to have to admit to herself. Especially while she was trapped here with him.

Especially while it felt a lot like the universe was giving her an opportunity to exorcise the actual demon that was hounding her.

The problem was that she had a job lined up with a man who certainly thought that she was coming to also have a physical relationship with him. And that, she supposed, was where Jericho's concern for her well-being in that regard had come from. She could suddenly see how very sticky it all was. Because if she slept with Jericho now...

Well, she wouldn't expect them to have a relationship. No. Far from that.

They could barely be in the same room without bickering. They were a very bad match, actually. It was just that she happened to be very particularly attracted to him. It was just that she couldn't imagine touching him and then... And then touching someone else.

Well, he has given no real indication that he wants to touch you, barring his strange and deep fascination with your virginal status.

It was true. He had not given a real indication that he wanted to touch her. Everything that she was thinking was based firmly in the realm of fantasy. Firmly in her head.

She started to open up the pantry doors and

search around for dry ingredients. She found a cookbook and was successful at finding the ingredients necessary for a quick bread. There was no yeast. And she supposed that was a gift. The Irish soda bread would be quick. And the odds of her screwing it up, even with the woodstove were low.

She was thankful now that her father had made her learn basic survival skills. And that he had made sure she knew how to keep a fire going.

And she just had to wonder…if what Jericho said was true. If what was happening with the winery didn't have anything to do with the fact that she was a girl, or the fact that her father doubted her competence. But everything to do with the fact that he was simply done. That it had become an albatross to him, and he had nothing left to prove.

She knew that the reason that he'd started the winery in the first place had been to get at James Maxfield, her sister-in-law's father, who had stolen the love of her father's life away from him many years ago.

Her father's obsession with proving that he was good enough had driven a wedge between her parents; at least, that was something that her father had been talking about lately. His own shortcomings. The ways that he hadn't managed to be the husband that he wanted to be because he was so lost in what could've been. The way that he had never really appreciated what he'd had.

He had the woman he'd always loved now, but she knew that getting there hadn't been the easiest of journeys.

So maybe that was it. Maybe he just couldn't separate his own feelings from the equation.

She mixed together all the dough, which in her opinion formed kind of an unattractive lump, and put it in a cast-iron skillet, which she then slipped into the oven.

She had no idea how to gauge the heat or the doneness in a wood fire oven, so she kept a continual eye on it. But much to her gratification, the smell that filled the kitchen was lovely.

By the time lunch rolled around she had a

beautiful-looking round of bread that she was ready to slather in butter.

But Jericho hadn't returned.

She felt the prickle of worry.

The snow was still coming down pretty hard outside, and while she didn't think he could've gotten lost, she didn't really know.

Neither of them knew this area, and the visibility was poor. She had no idea where the wood was that he was supposed to go chop. And he might've injured himself. It was icy outside. Him walking in the ice with an ax was a whole different thing to concern herself with.

And it just didn't matter how fine everything seemed. She knew that better than most.

Good people were taken away for no reason. All the time.

No one was safe. Nothing was truly protected from harm.

With a bit of panic building in her breast, she grabbed her coat and slipped out the front door.

The silence was eerie. All noise insulated

by the dense cover of snow all around. It was still falling, and every so often she would hear a tree groan beneath the weight of it.

That was another thing to worry about. Falling trees and limbs. The snow here was so wet that it fell heavy and thick on the branches. And could easily create a disaster. Downed power lines and trees, mudslides...

She sucked in a sharp breath and regretted it, when the cold touched the back of her throat and made her cough.

It was so cold.

Snow like this was such a rarity that she really wasn't used to it. They got a light dusting now and again down in Gold Valley, but anything thicker and heavier typically fell up in the mountains, where she did not live. So it was just all very unusual.

She would like to enjoy the novelty a little bit, but it was essentially impossible, given that the novelty was pretty well stripped away by the reality of the situation.

She paused for a moment and heard a loud crack. One that she hoped was the sound of

Jericho chopping wood, and not the sound of a tree limb giving way.

She scrambled that direction, slipping and sliding in the slushy snow that went past her knees.

Her boots were insufficient, and snow went over the edges, down into her feet.

She shivered. But she kept on going.

She heard the crack again and was reasonably certain that it had to be Jericho. But she pressed on anyway.

She came up over a snowy ridge and saw him, swinging the ax and bringing it down unerringly on the log piece, splitting it in two.

Then he dropped the ax, and picked up the stack of wood that he had produced, lifting it easily and beginning to walk up the hill. He stopped when he saw her.

"What the hell are you doing?"

"I came looking for you."

"It's freezing," he said.

"Yes, I know. It's why I was worried about you. I'm fine." Except for the snow in her boots.

"You don't look fine."

"I am." But her teeth began to chatter.

"March yourself back to the house."

"I was worried about you," she said. He walked up the hill, and she waited for him to reach her. He was laden with wood.

"I can take some of that."

"No, you can't. Go on."

"I could," she insisted.

"Your feet are about to fall off. Don't tell me those boots are waterproof."

"Fine. They're not. But my feet are not going to fall off."

"Go."

"There are fires and everything back at the house," she protested. "I'll be fine."

"This isn't a joke," he said. "I understand that we landed ourselves in a really cushy situation, but this is the kind of weather that kills people, Honey, and you were worried about that when we were stuck by the side of the road, but I feel like you're not as worried about as you should be now."

"Oh no, that's not fair. Because I went out

looking for you because I was afraid that something happened to you. Because I know that this is the kind of weather that kills people."

"And if you found me, what were you going to do? Were you going to carry me back to the cabin?"

She looked up, all the way up, so she could meet his gaze. "Yeah. I think I could have."

"You think that you could've carried me back. Through the snow."

"Women lift cars and stuff when their children are in trouble. I'm pretty sure that I could drag you if I had the kind of adrenaline that… Well, I'm sure it's less adrenaline than a woman needing to lift the car off her child. But I bet it's an appropriate amount to move you."

"You're infuriating."

"How am I infuriating?"

"Because you keep overestimating yourself. You keep acting like you know the way of the world when you damn well don't. You don't know the state of anything, Honey. You just don't. You don't know as much as you think you do, you don't…"

"I'm fine. I made bread."

"No. You're acting like a child. Because why? Because you're mad that I have the winery?"

"Because I am furious," she said. "Because I'm furious that you have the winery, and that I had been fixated on your ass for at least ten years. It is ridiculous, and I'm over it. How can I… How can I want you when you are such a jerk, and I don't even like you."

He looked like she had picked up a ball of that wet snow and hit him in the face with it.

And she realized that she'd said it. She had actually said it. And it was more awful and horrible than the revelation of her virginity ever could have been.

"Oh…"

"What do you mean you want me?"

"It's just that…" She stopped.

"Don't stop," he said. "Your feet are wet. Explain yourself."

She felt she was being frog-marched through

the snow, and she had gone and embarrassed herself so deeply that she was sweaty along with freezing. Which was just a terrible combination. And it couldn't get any worse.

So some small part of her felt compelled to try to *make it worse.*

"I'll explain myself… It's just… I wanted to sleep with somebody else to get away from you. And to get away from the way that you make me feel. And to get away from…everything."

They arrived back at the house and he opened the door, propelling her inside. "Go take your clothes off."

"What?" It came out as a squeak.

"You heard me."

"I… I said that I… I didn't say that I wanted to…"

"We'll deal with that later. Right now you need to get warm. There's a sauna outside. Get those boots off, strip yourself down and put on the robe in the bathroom. I'll start the sauna."

"Oh… But don't you want to…"

"What I want is for your feet to not fall off," he said. "That's what I want. The rest of all this running off at the mouth you're doing we'll deal with later. But right now, you keeping your feet is the important thing."

Shivering, she shut herself in the bathroom and looked at the shower. She knew that it theoretically had hot water. She could just refuse to do what he said and get in the shower. But instead, she found herself stripping down and putting on the thick robe that was hung there. There were a pair of boots that looked soft and fuzzy, and the label over the top said sauna slippers.

She slipped her feet into them. They were lined with wool, and appeared to have a treated, waterproof exterior.

When she exited the bathroom, Jericho was nowhere to be seen, and it was probably all for the best, because she was naked beneath the robe and it made her feel uncomfortable, even though she was naked beneath all of her clothes, if she thought too deeply about it.

She picked up the paper that had all the directions for the house and saw that it stated there was a map on the back. She flipped it over and saw a hand-drawn guide to how to get to the sauna.

She shuffled out into the snow, thankfully not into any parts that were as deep as where she'd been a little earlier. So her feet stayed dry.

She saw smoke coming out of the top and was curious. She did not know how an off-grid sauna worked.

She opened up the door and Jericho was inside, his jacket cast to the side, his shirt-sleeves rolled up as he fed wood chips into the fire. Then he took a ladle and poured water over the hot rocks at the top of the stove, steam coming off them in waves.

"This is how you do it," he said, pouring more water over it.

It was already toasty inside.

"And you need it."

"Thanks," she said.

She had closed the door behind her, because leaving it open seemed... Well, it seemed counter to the point of getting the sauna warm. But now she realized that she had gone and enclosed herself in a very tight space with the very man she was feeling completely self-conscious about.

And also that she was wearing only a robe.

"If you're in here for longer than twenty minutes, I'm going to come looking for you."

"Right."

Wherein she would be naked.

She shifted uncomfortably, heat building between her legs. Why was it like this? Why was it so...

It wasn't inevitable. She wanted it to be. And that was the problem. She was so hung up on him that she was pushing in a direction that she probably shouldn't go.

But all this... All this blurting she was doing, she didn't actually think that it was organic. She was obviously pushing the conversation. Holding herself back from saying the thing that she actually wanted, but saying everything but.

The fact of the matter was, what she really

wanted was for him to be her first. What she really wanted was for him to be the one to introduce her to…to sex.

Because for all that he infuriated her, he was the only man that she had practically ever really wanted. He was the only man that she could really imagine herself being with. And imagine it she had. Repeatedly. In vivid detail.

Her chest felt tight, and her whole body flushed.

And then suddenly, she realized. She was going to do it. She was going to do it, become it, because she had already embarrassed herself. She had already told him that she was a virgin. She had already told him that she wanted him. She was just going to do this.

So she reached down to the belt of the robe and undid it. Then she let it drop to the floor. And she was standing before him, wearing nothing other than ridiculous shearling boots and a smile.

"Maybe you could stay." Her voice felt scratchy; she felt scratchy. Her heart was pounding so hard she could barely hear, and the steam filling up the room seemed to swallow her voice.

But she could see his face. She could see the tightness there. The intensity.

"Honey…"

"No. I just… Maybe this is the time to have a conversation, actually. The one that we decided to have later. Because I'm getting warm. I'm very warm."

"Put your robe back on."

"What if I don't want to?"

"Why not?"

"Because I want you. I already admitted to that. Why do you think I'm so upset? All the time? About all the women that you bring into the winery, about the fact that my father gave it to you. About the fact that we're stuck together, but will never actually be together. And that's why I had to leave. I'm not an idiot, Jericho, I know that you and I are never going to… We're not going to fall in love and get married. We can hardly stand to be in the same room as each other. But I have wanted you since I understood what that meant. And I don't know what to do about it. Short of running away and having sex with someone else. That was my game plan. My game plan was to go off and have sex with another man. And that got thwarted. You were the one that picked me up. You're the one that I'm stuck here with in the snow. And I'm not going to claim that it's fate. Because I can feel myself twisting every single element of this except for the weather. The blizzard isn't my fault. But I'm making the choice to go ahead and offer... Me."

"I..."

"If you're going to reject me, just don't do it horribly."

And then suddenly, she found herself being tugged into his arms, the heat from his body more intense than the heat from the sauna, the roughness of his clothes a shock against her skin. And then his mouth crashed down on hers.

Seven

He was being an idiot. He was being a damned idiot. There were so many women out there in the world that he could sleep with and suffer no consequences for doing so. She was not one of them. She was in fact one of the few women who wasn't in that number. The only others were his friends' wives. And then there was Honey. And she was clinging to him like she wanted him. Like she wanted him and needed him. Like he was air.

He'd tried to resist. He'd told himself to. But she wanted him.

That changed everything.

And she was so damn soft. And he was powerless not to rub his hands up and down her curves. From her rib cage just beneath her breasts, down her slender waist, to cup her ass, which was the most delightful handful he could've imagined.

And back up again. She was divine. And sweet. Just like her name suggested.

She might be vinegar when she talked, but when she kissed…

She shivered in his hold, her response to his kisses so intense it floored him. She was trembling with need. And it was… It was intoxicating. And maybe because she was a woman that he shouldn't want, he wanted her all the more. Maybe that's what made her skin so soft. Maybe that's what made her cries of pleasure so sweet. Maybe that was what made her so damned irresistible.

He moved both hands down to her ass and squeezed her tight, pulling her up against him so that she could feel how hard he was. And he knew it was too late. Knew that it was too late for better judgment and smarter decisions. There was no decision to be made. She was naked, she was in his arms and he wanted her.

He lifted her up off the ground, sat down on the wooden bench there in the sauna with her legs parted wide, her thighs on either side of his. He tilted his head back and looked at her, as best he could in the steamy room. Her breasts were small and round, beautiful, her nipples the same color as her name.

Tight and begging for his attention. Her stomach was flat, muscled from all the hard labor that she did, her thighs just the same. And that thatch of curls between her legs... It was all he could have ever asked for.

He gripped her hips, stared at the way his hands looked against her skin, moved them up beneath her breasts and slid his thumb across her nipples. She was beautiful. Delicious. He leaned forward and kissed her, right between her breasts, and she arched.

"Tell me if you want me to stop," he said, his voice rough.

"Don't stop," she whispered. "Please don't stop."

He lowered his head and sucked one bud into his mouth, flooded with relief. Because all this tension that had existed inside of him had suddenly unwound, tension he had known was there.

The denial that he wanted this. The denial that he wanted her. He did. And there was no denying it or hiding it. He had tried. He had put it down to a few errant moments of looking at her ass, but it was a hell of a lot more than that.

It had been building. And he knew it. It was why he'd been so furious when she said she was going to sleep with someone. It was why he'd been so obsessed when he'd found out that she hadn't.

Because he was full of this. This deep, dark, forbidden desire for a woman that he knew he wasn't supposed to touch.

But he was touching her now. Tasting her.

And it was a hell of a thing.

He moved his head from her first breast and

then paid equal attention to the other, where she was just as sweet, just as filled with desire for him. She let her head fall back, and a cry of need escaped her mouth.

He didn't have a condom in here, so it wasn't going to go all the way. But he could take her there.

He curved his forearms up beneath her knees, pressed his hands to her lower back and lifted her from his lap as he slowly laid her down across the bench, parting her thighs and gazing at all of her feminine beauty.

"Jericho," she whispered.

She said his name. She said that she wanted him.

This seemed to prove it. Beautifully.

This was insanity. But he was neck-deep in it and feeling fine. Feeling ready to be submersed. He kissed her inner thigh, and she shuddered. Then he lowered his head, flicking his tongue over the source of her pleasure.

She gasped, arching against his mouth.

And she tasted sweet, and he knew that he

had overdone it on the references to Honey, but it kept being true.

And he didn't know how he had ever thought of her as simply Creed and Jackson's younger sister. She was Honey and herself. And right now, she felt a whole lot like his. Right now, he didn't want to think of what moment followed this one, where she was so perfectly sweet and aroused for him. Only for him. All for him.

So he kissed her there, and teased her, until she was writhing against him, until she was begging.

Until she was crying out her pleasure, and he could feel it. Deep down inside. He could feel it.

"Jericho," she gasped.

The scene was all around them, between them. And she sat up. She looked dazed, filled with wonder. Her skin was dewy from the heat and the steam, and he wanted to lick every inch of her. And he had never seen a more beautiful sight.

Forbidden fruit. Pleasure deferred. Whatever you wanted to call it. It was damn sweet.

"Jericho…" And then suddenly she basically flung herself at him, kissing him, touching his chest, and he was so hard it hurt. She settled herself on his lap, the slick, wet heat of her hot against his denim-covered arousal.

He moved his hands over her curves, over her softness. And he knew that he would never get enough. Not of her. Not of this. Ever.

It was a scary thought, considering he shouldn't even have another bite, let alone gorge himself on the feast like he wanted to.

"I don't have a condom," he said.

"I have tons of condoms," she said.

"I meant I don't have a condom in here."

"Right," she said. "Oh… Oh. But we should get one."

"We should go back to the house."

"To get a condom."

"Maybe to take a breath," he said. But he would rather have a condom.

"I don't want to take a breath."

And she was looking at him expectantly, and he realized if he stopped now it would be… Well, it would be because of something other than her.

Sure, some of it was because of him. Some of it was because he was the last man who should be taking someone's virginity. He didn't have the sensitivity for that. He didn't have the sensitivity or the emotional… Anything. To be the person who should be handling something like this. But a lot of it was about Creed and Jackson, and at the end of the day, that wasn't fair. Because Honey was her own person, and the fact that her family seemed dedicated to not treating her like her own person, capable of making her own decisions, not even bothering to check with her before her dad sold the winery… All of that… That was… Well, it wasn't fair. She deserved to be treated like she knew her own mind.

Right. And that's the thing that will get you laid.

He wasn't going to claim he was being altruistic about it. But he was looking at it from a different angle. That was all.

The angle that let him have an orgasm.

But no. It would never just be that. She would never just be that. She was Honey Cooper, and he wasn't going to pretend otherwise. If he wanted to get laid, he could get laid. But she said she'd always wanted him. She'd said…

Well. You're a little bit sad.

Because the fact that she'd always wanted him, that meant something to *him*. This girl, this beautiful woman, who was part of the best family he'd ever known, wanted him. He couldn't deny that did something to him. Made something inside of him that had previously felt shattered feel fixed. And the fact that he wanted to chase some feeling of redemption in her arms was messed up as hell. The fact that he seemed to believe on some level that the gift of her body was going to wash away a world of hurt… Yeah, well, he had never claimed to be the most emotionally well-balanced person. Quite the opposite. He knew that he was a mess. He'd always known.

The kid who'd never really been a kid. The kid who'd been rejected by his father. Who'd lost his mother. Yeah, he never claimed to be real balanced. So he might as well just embrace it. Because hell, they were snowed in. What else could they do? And he could turn away from it now, but the odds of them resisting were low. Unless they were going to be rescued in the next ten minutes, and the way the snow continued to come down didn't make it seem likely—well, he might as well just go with it.

So he wrapped her in the robe, scooped her up in his arms, realized that she had never taken those boots off and pushed open the door to the sauna. It was still freezing cold outside. The snow was continuing to dump down in buckets, and he didn't know how long they would be stuck here.

"This is an extraordinary circumstance," he said, carrying them both through the snow. "And when we get rescued…"

"Right," she said. "I get it. Only during the snowstorm."

"Only during the snowstorm."

"What if we end up here for Christmas?"

"I don't know. I guess we'll cross that bridge when we come to it."

"I would like to cross this other bridge first."

"Seems like a good idea to me."

He kicked open the door to the cabin, then closed it behind him with his heel. They would need to get a fire going again in the bedroom.

He carried her up the stairs, and she clung to him, her arms around his neck, and her eyes took on a strange, soft look.

"What?"

"Well," she said. "No one has ever… I mean… No one has ever treated me like this. I had to be tough pretty much this whole time."

She had been. Tough, mouthy Honey, and everybody did treat her that way. He knew that was so. Even he was guilty of it. But did nobody really treat her with any softness? That was all he wanted to do. Wrap her in furs and make sure she was warm. Well, that was not all he wanted to do, but it was definitely the more gentlemanly thing he wanted to do.

He hadn't felt compelled to care for anyone in years. He'd been burned out on it. But Honey always seemed so invulnerable. And he knew she wasn't. That much had become clear on this little trip together.

It brought out tenderness in him he'd thought long gone.

He didn't say anything. Instead, he just kissed her. He kissed her because she was beautiful. He kissed her because he wanted her to feel that.

He kissed her because there weren't words to say that he was sorry for all the softness she'd missed out on because her mother had died. Because she had then been surrounded by people who were as wounded and hard and hurt as she was.

That was the truth of it. They had taken him

in, but they were all in the same boat. Grieving and wretched and in general some of the least emotionally conversant people around.

And they'd all been there for each other, but clearly something was missing. For her.

Something no one had realized.

He would make it his mission for her to feel it here. For her to feel it this week. *Week. You don't know how long it's going to be.*

No. He didn't.

Someone could come knocking on the door right now—which he found he really didn't want—someone could find them in a week. Two weeks. They might be able to get the car out in the next couple of days. They didn't know.

But right now, it didn't matter. Right now, he was determined to dedicate everything in his power to making Honey feel all the things that she hadn't before.

That's a power trip.

Maybe. Maybe it was a power trip. Because he was a kid who—at the end of the day—felt like he had never really been able to offer much to anyone. He had tried, but his mother had still died. His father hadn't been there. The Coopers had given to him. And in the end, he felt like, to an extent, he had given back by buying the winery. Except he had still hurt Honey. And that did matter.

Sure, his own success was important. But so was her happiness.

And for the first time, he felt like he might be giving more than he was taking, and that was a pretty good feeling. Even if it was trumped up, all things considered. Since he was also getting sex and it wasn't like this was a mission of charity.

He was hardly the Mother Teresa of orgasms.

The bedroom was cold, and he laid her out gingerly on the bed and wrapped her up in the furs there.

She burrowed beneath them happily and kept her eyes on him as he began to build the fire.

The urge that he had to suddenly just… give her everything that he could think of…

It was almost overpowering. He wanted her to have…every good thing. Every good thing. He got the fire going, nice and big, and when it was done, he straightened. "Okay. So tell me where the condoms are."

Eight

Honey fought the urge to burrow deeper beneath the covers. She was... She was so desperately aroused, so desperately excited that she could barely breathe. Jericho had kissed her. Well, she had kissed him. After stripping naked. And then he had... Hell. He had kissed her. And places that she hadn't even got around to fantasizing he might kiss her.

It had been transformative. And now this. This realization of her deepest fantasy. She wanted this man. She wanted this man in ways that defied her experience. That far outstripped anything she'd ever done, anything she'd ever fantasized about in a concrete fashion.

It was real. But it was ephemeral and unformed. A mass of feelings that made her breath quicken and made her heart beat faster.

He was beautiful. She had always thought so. But it was the way he looked at her. That was what truly left her in awe. That was what made it so she couldn't think.

Because he wasn't looking at her like she was just Honey, the same woman that he'd seen every day for the past who knew how many years. He was looking at her like he'd never really seen her before. And that made her feel new. The kind of new that she had wanted. The kind of new that she had believed might be out there for her, but it was better than finding it with a man she had never met before. She had found it with him.

She had found it with him, and she hadn't been expecting that.

Oh, how she wanted this man, this man who looked at her as if he had never seen her before, all the while he was a man who saw her all the time.

It was the fulfillment of her deepest need. Her deepest fantasy.

He was everything.

But she was nervous. And she found herself shrinking into those furs and that soft mattress.

They had shared this bed last night, but they had kept a healthy amount of space between them. Just a few moments ago in the sauna there had been nothing between them at all. And now...

"Are you okay?"

"Yes," she said, doing her best to sound emphatic.

It came out with just a little more tremble than she would've liked.

"Are you sure?"

"I am absolutely sure. I did say."

"You can always change your mind."

In those words, coming from the strongest, hottest man she had ever known, who was essentially sex and cowboy boots, did something to fire up her arousal even more.

He was strong enough to take what he wanted, to do whatever he wanted. He was strong enough to break her if he wanted to, but he didn't want that. He wanted to use his hands to give her pleasure, and only the pleasure that she wanted.

He was more than any fantasy she'd ever had. And she was so unbearably aware, not of his strength then, but of the way that he kept it leashed.

That was power. And the intensity of it was enough to make her combust.

"I am 100 percent sure that I want to have sex with you, Jericho. I have been 100 percent sure of that for a very long time."

"And yet you're so mean to me."

"It didn't stop you from wanting to have sex with me," she pointed out. And then she suddenly became very afraid that he didn't actually want to have sex with her. What if she was just a charity case? What if this was just pity? Or worse, some misguided overprotective instinct because he didn't want her to have sex with a man she didn't know, a man that she was going to go work for. What if this was…him using his penis as a protective shield. Like parents who wanted their kids to drink at home if they were going to drink. Maybe he wanted her to have sex with him if she was going to have sex with anyone.

That would just be a whole lot of a hot mess. And she did not want that.

Except she didn't really want to question him either. Because she wanted him. But of course, him not really wanting her would be unbearable…

"Is this about me? I mean, at all? Do you… Are you attracted to me?"

He huffed a laugh. "I have spent the last little bit trying not to notice just how beautiful you were. Because the fact of the matter is, there's a lot of women that I could be with who don't present as much of a complication as you do."

"That is not very flattering," she said, wrinkling her nose.

"I'm not trying to flatter you. I'm trying to be honest with you. And honestly? This is a terrible idea. If your brothers find out, they're going to kick my ass. Your dad's gonna kick my ass. Hell, maybe when I come to my senses, I'm going to want to kick my own ass. But I want you more than I care about that."

He hesitated for a second. As if there was something else he wanted to say, but then he didn't.

"All this is insulting, and deeply flattering at the same time. I'll take it." Because her chest burned. With satisfaction. With triumph. With the knowledge and desire that whether or not she was a terrible idea, Jericho Smith wanted her. He could have any woman. Fundamentally, he often did.

But right now he wanted her. Right now, she was the thing that he craved. Right now, she wanted to luxuriate in that more than just about anything. "The condoms are in my suitcase."

"The lingerie suitcase."

"Yes. I have several boxes, and I bought

different kinds. Because I didn't know… You know, they say ribbed on some of them. And I didn't really know what that meant, so I got that. But I got regular kinds too." She felt silly all of a sudden.

"As long as they're not hot pink, I'm fine."

"What if they are? Would that be a deal breaker?"

He shifted. "At this point, nothing is a deal breaker. I'm too far gone."

The fact that he couldn't reject her over a hot pink condom was another spurious compliment, but another one that she would gladly take.

He got up close to the suitcase and bent down in front of it, taking out a couple of boxes. "Did you choose the ribbed?"

"No."

"Why not?"

"Because I think I can manage your pleasure just fine without them." His lips hitched upward into a grin that made her stomach flip. "In fact. I know I can."

"You are very confident. Has anyone ever told you that before?"

"Yeah. Though, usually the word is *arrogant*."

"You don't sound bothered by it."

"The question I always have about arrogance is why is it a problem if you can back all your claims up?" He grinned. "Am I arrogant? Or am I just telling the truth."

"I feel that I will not be able to comment upon that until after... After."

"If you're still able to comment after, I'll consider it a personal failure."

He took a whole strip of the condoms from the box, dropped it back into the suitcase, then deposited the protection on the end of the bed. Then he stood there, pitched his cowboy hat up off his head and pulled his shirt up directly after.

Her mouth went dry. She knew that he was beautiful. She had known. But the last time she had seen him shirtless, it had been all fruitless longing and furtive, embarrassed attempts to keep herself from staring too intently. And now she just looked her fill. Because why not? Why not just look? His dark brown skin, with hard ridged muscles and just the right amount of dark hair was the perfect representation of all things masculine. And it called to everything feminine in her. To her softness. A softness that she'd had to deny more than indulge, because she had been dropped into a world that was hard. A world she knew was hard.

And all of her soft feelings had always felt twisted around that reality. Around the truth that there was no reward for being sad or grieving, and there was no special prize for having lost much in life. She'd made the mistake of getting lost in all that once, and she'd only caused other people grief.

So she had just done her best to cover it up, to get along.

And it had all come to a head in an explosion of anger when her father had sold him the winery, but there was just so much more to her than that. So much more to her than anger. And she didn't often let herself explore that or feel that. And maybe that was partly why her attraction to him had often come out as an expression of anger or aggression. Because it was easier. Because if it wasn't that, it was softness. And it was the softness she had always feared. But there was something about him, and all that masculine hardness that made her want to luxuriate in everything about herself that was different.

And she found herself slipping out from under the covers. Not quite so embarrassed now to show herself. She kicked the boots off beneath the blankets and shoved them down off the edge of the mattress, then slipped out from beneath the furs, parting her robe as she did. Exposing her breasts on a rush of air. She had done the same thing in the sauna, but she had felt insulated by the steam then. But there was nothing concealing her now. The firelight glowed over his skin and hers. And it added to the intimacy of it. To the mood. To the magic of the moment.

She climbed out from beneath the covers

completely, slipping the robe away, showing him her.

He sucked in a harsh breath through his teeth. "You are so damn sexy."

He saw *her.*

Not what she had been able to show the world up until this point. Not the things her brothers wanted other people to see, or that her father thought. He saw her. A piece of herself that she wasn't even fully comfortable with. Because even when she had made the decision to go up north and sleep with Donovan, she hadn't been driven by an overwhelming surge of attraction. Or by being in touch with her sexuality. Rather it had been anger. Just more anger, fueling her and firing her on. And right now she wasn't angry. Right now, she was soft and she was vulnerable, and if he said something pointed, she had a feeling that he could rent her in two.

But he wasn't. Instead, he had said just the right thing. Just the perfect thing. Instead, he had made her feel like more, not less.

She was very unbearably conscious just

then of all the things that she had missed in her life because she hadn't had a mother.

The conversations, the shopping trips. She wondered if her mother would've shifted her focus just enough so that this feminine piece of herself didn't feel quite so foreign.

So that her focus hadn't been so squarely on simply fitting in with her family. Because there would've been someone else like her. Someone else who was different. And maybe she would've still been the same her, but maybe the feminine mystique wouldn't have been quite so…mystical.

It didn't feel mystical now. It felt simple.

But she was safe with him. The stranger who was also familiar.

He put his hands on his belt, while he kicked his boots off and shrugged off his jeans and underwear in one fluid motion. Her mouth went dry.

Because in his entirety, he was the most gorgeous thing she had ever seen.

A friend of hers in high school—just a casual friend—had once said that she had seen a penis in person and was not going to rush to buy artistic renderings of it for her room.

She really thought that she might buy some art if it was fashioned to look like him.

He was art all on his own. Thick and strong and large.

His thighs were muscular, his waist lean, every ounce of hard work that man did etched deep into his muscles.

He was a sculpture come to life, every loving detail on his body seemingly handcrafted into an ideal human form.

She had done a bit of time on the internet, trying to prepare herself for what was going to happen. Not with porn, obviously—she knew better than to try to consult male fantasies for what she should expect out of sex. But she had done a bit of reading on how sometimes the first time hurt—but probably not if the woman was a little older and had ridden a lot of horses—she qualified as an older virgin, and she had certainly done her fair share of horse riding.

She also knew—because she wasn't a child—that a man would fit.

But right now, inexplicably, she felt a bit nervous about that. Just a bit skeptical. But then he came down on the bed beside her, and he was kissing her, the length of his naked body pressed against hers, and she forgot to be nervous. She forgot everything but the way that it felt to be touched by him. Kissed by him.

And suddenly, ridiculously, her eyes filled with tears. Because this was… It was different than she had imagined it would be. He was different. There was no fighting, no banter, no ridiculousness. None of the things that they threw out between each other to keep the other distant. That was what she did. All the time. Throwing down gauntlets and throwing out outrageous statements to keep him standing back. So that she wasn't challenged. So that he didn't see.

But he could see now. And he knew. He knew that she wanted him. And the world hadn't collapsed in on itself. Rather, a whole new world had opened up to her. Rather, everything had become brighter and brilliant and more beautiful.

And, oh, how she wanted him.

She was on fire with it. That heat between her legs slick and hot and ready.

As if on cue, he put his hand there, between her thighs, rubbing at the sensitive bundle of nerves there. And she arched against him. He pushed a finger inside of her tight channel, and she winced.

Okay. Maybe the horse riding wasn't going to make this as easy as she'd hoped.

But then he pushed another finger in and kept on kissing her. And she got wetter and hotter, and if there was still pain, it didn't matter quite so much. If there was still pain, it didn't surpass the deep, throbbing need inside of her. She burned.

And he was the only thing that could possibly put out the fire. Or maybe he would simply be gasoline on a lit match. Maybe he would still get higher, and maybe that was what she wanted. To burn out of control with no end in sight.

He teased her and toyed with her until the pleasure built to unbearable heights. Until her entire world reduced to his mouth on hers and his fingers inside her.

And then she shattered. Her climax rolling over her like a wave. And when she came back to herself, he was positioned between her thighs, the protection firmly in place.

"I'm ready," she said.

And he thrust home. Deep and hard. She gasped, arching against him. She was overwhelmed by the sensation of fullness, but it wasn't bad.

No. It wasn't bad. It was him. Overwhelming and far too much, but the alternative was not having him, and that was simply something that she couldn't take. A reality that she wouldn't be happy with at all.

And then, he began to move, the fullness becoming essential rather than unbearable, the weight of him a gift that she wanted to hang on to forever. Impossibly, she felt another climax begin to build. This went deeper, more intense than the previous two. Her body tightened around his, and she arched her back, throwing her head back against the pillows, crying out her pleasure. And that was when he gave himself over to it. Lost himself in his own desire. And all the while she was still riding out the aftershocks of her desire, she was flooded by the overwhelming satisfaction of his.

She had never been with a man before. And he had been with plenty of women. But they were shaking just the same. She was clinging to him, his body sweat slicked, his desire so apparent, and she felt...

She felt more herself than she ever had in her life.

She had done it. She was no longer a virgin. But she realized that wasn't even what mattered. What mattered was him.

She pushed that realization aside as quickly as it occurred, because of all the things that could potentially ruin this, that was the worst.

This was just for the blizzard.

It was great that it could be him. Because she had always wanted him, but she didn't need him to be essential. In fact she needed him to very much not be. He was hot, and she liked him. And without feeling the need to distance him because of her attraction to him, they would probably feel like they liked each other even more.

But it could only ever be this. This cold weather thing. That would melt along with the snow.

She chose not to think about that. Instead, she snuggled against him beneath the furs. She thought about saying something. There was nothing to say. And sleep was dragging her under.

So she gave in to it. For the first time in memory Honey Cooper just didn't bother to fight. Instead, she just rested.

Nine

"I told you," Jericho said when Honey's eyes finally fluttered open. "If you still had something to say then I wasn't worthy of my arrogance."

She gazed at him out of her narrowed eyes. "That is really the first thing on your mind?"

"Yes, ma'am. I'm always on hand for the 'I told you so.'"

"That is deeply, deeply petty."

"I never said I wasn't." And all right, it wasn't the most romantic thing. But they weren't romantic.

Except... She had been amazing, and he was getting impatient watching her sleep. It was the middle of the day, after all.

And you want her again.

Not that he could afford to. Not that either of them could afford this.

But hey, they were stuck here until the weather cleared, which it still hadn't done. And as long as they could make the most of it, why shouldn't they? As long as they were here...

"Well, fine. You have earned your arrogance."

"Happy to hear it."

Her stomach growled. Audibly. "I'm hungry."

He was too. But not particularly for food.

"You can have some food. After you have a bath."

"Hey," she said, as he picked her up out of the bed. "I can walk, you know. You seem to have forgotten that."

"I didn't forget. I just like carrying you."

It was true.

He liked the feeling of the soft weight in his arms. He liked feeling her in general.

"I'll get you your bird book if you want."

"I don't want the bird book."

He chuckled. "How about I take a bath with you?"

A flush covered her skin, and he was ridiculously pleased by it. That she was affected by them. By this.

You've lost your mind.

Maybe. But it didn't seem so crazy that what he wanted was to stay here, not face what was out there. Not deal with the fact that he had a long-lost family he was supposed to be spending Christmas with. Yeah, spending time with Honey was a hell of a lot nicer.

He had run the bath already, because he hadn't been totally sure that they would have enough hot water, and it had been pretty close. He'd warmed a couple pots up on the stove and added them to the deep claw-foot tub in the bathroom.

He deposited her in the warm water and watched the way the firelight sparkled over her damp skin. She was so damned pretty. So perfect. It made him feel… Well, it made him feel a damn sight too much. "Good," he said. But she didn't move at all, and he laughed as he got into the tub and lifted her, setting her back down so that she was on his lap.

She sighed, letting her head fall back against his chest. Then she tilted her head. Looking at him as best she could. "This is very strange."

"How so?" But it made his chest tight.

"Well, just a few hours ago we were fully clothed and sitting across the room from each other talking about birds…"

"I never really talked about birds. It was mostly you talking about birds."

"Whatever," she said. "It's just that… It's very strange to now be sitting with you like this. Without clothes."

And perhaps the strangest part of all was it didn't feel strange. Because they were still them. She was still talking about birds.

"Right."

He lifted his hand from the water, let the droplets fall over her skin. Her breasts.

He was transfixed by the sight of her. By her beauty. And he hadn't gotten to where he was marinating in the strangeness of it, because he wanted her for as long as he had and now he finally had her.

She was as beautiful as he'd imagined that she might be. And that was... Well, his imagination had been pretty thorough, but it still hadn't quite managed to get the particulars. Every dip and hollow and facet of beauty that was unique to Honey.

It was strange. The rightness of it.

"Yeah. I guess," he said, even though he didn't feel the same disquiet he imagined she did. Perhaps it was experience.

Except he knew it wasn't that. Maybe it was just the way they were cocooned in this moment. The entire thing had been a little bit surreal. Maybe he had just sunk into it. Maybe he'd been sinking into it for the last month, finding out the Daltons didn't know about him—or at least Hank hadn't. That he actually wanted to get to know him.

"It's only a few days before Christmas," he said.

What was supposed to have been his first Christmas with his father.

A father. What does that even mean when you find out when you are thirty-four years old?

What did it mean at all? He hadn't been there for anything. He hadn't been there to help Jericho when everything had fallen apart.

Whether or not it was his choice didn't really matter, because the end result was the same.

And joining the family now… It was kind of the ninth inning. He didn't need their support. Not anymore.

He figured out how to get along. He figured it out on his own. That he felt compelled to go… Well, maybe it was a good thing that he hit a snowstorm.

After all, he was here, naked with Honey,

rather than dealing with the awkwardness of the family situation.

"We need a Christmas tree," she whispered.

"A Christmas tree?" There was weight that came with that, baggage and pain that he didn't want to think about now.

But Honey wanted a Christmas tree, and he found that he wanted to please her. It was such a strange sensation. One lost way back in time.

"Yes, Jericho," she said, oblivious to his inner turmoil. "So that we can have a Merry Christmas."

"I didn't get you anything," he said.

She laughed. "I think you did."

"Well, I'm not the kind of man who would say that a couple of orgasms for me were a gift."

That made her howl, slapping the surface of the water. "Since when?"

"All right, I am." Something sincere rose up inside of him, and he didn't quite know what to do with it. It was just that… For her that didn't seem like enough. He wanted there to be more. He wanted to give her something, and the impulse felt strange and foreign. The impulse felt undeniable.

It was the strangest damn thing.

"All right, how about a Christmas tree then? And maybe I can find a really pretty rock to wrap up for you."

"And what will you wrap it in?" she asked, smiling sweetly.

He smiled back, but it was wicked. "Maybe some of those lace panties that you brought."

She snickered, readjusting herself, her bottom moving over his growing arousal. He really needed to give her a break. She had been a virgin. And it was very likely that she could be sore.

If you had gotten her a nice enough gift, you might not have felt so guilty about her being sore.

Well, damn. That didn't say great things about them, but it was true. Because he wanted her again, soreness or not.

"All right," he said. "I'd rather see you in

the panties. Though, I'd also rather see you out of them."

"That is something I don't really understand about lingerie," she said. "Are you supposed to dress up in another room and make a grand entrance? And then you just put it on so it gets taken off thirty seconds later."

"You could put it on in front of me right now, take it off fifteen seconds later, and I would still think the whole thing was worth it, because it was just all staring at you."

Her cheeks went red. "Really?"

"Yes. Because you're so damn hot I can hardly deal with myself."

"Wow."

"What?"

"Nothing. Just..." She looked up at him with wide, sincere eyes that damn near broke his heart. "You really *do* think I'm hot?"

That question, so artless, sat like a weight in his chest, along with Christmas trees. "I really do. I wouldn't say it if I didn't think it."

"How long?"

"Why do you need to know how long?"

She turned over, a slippery mermaid in his arms, then rested her forearms against his chest and looked up at him. "I need to know because I have had the biggest crush on you for most of my life, all the while wanting to hit you over the head with the nearest blunt object. You are both my favorite and least favorite person to be around, often during the same conversation. And I have felt like a fool for feeling that way this whole time."

That admission stole his breath. He was older, and he might not have felt that way about her back when she did, but it wasn't because she wasn't…wonderful. It was because of their age gap. "Why did you feel that way? Like you were foolish for wanting me?"

"Because I just never thought that I was all that interesting or pretty or anything of the kind. I always felt a little bit on the outside in school. And I tried not to, but… I did. Beatrix Leighton gave me a mouse once. When we were in kindergarten. I kept him as a pet for three years. I thought that was one of the nicest things anyone ever did for me. I think she was about the closest I ever got to feeling like somebody might understand me. But she was usually nursing animals back to health and not doing anything social. But I just always felt like I didn't really fit. And..."

"I think everybody feels that way sometimes."

"Yeah?"

He smiled. "There aren't a whole lot of people who look like me around here."

"No, I know," she said. She looked away.

"Hey, don't be embarrassed. It's fine that you don't just think of it. But it is true. I get it. I know what it's like to feel different. But I also know what it's like to find people who get you. Who see past the obvious surface things and know you. Understand you."

"I don't know if anyone's ever actually understood me. I mean, my dad, Creed and Jackson, they all lost my mother, just like I did. And you lost your mother. You're about the closest anyone could ever come to understanding exactly what I've been through. But I think the thing that gets me is that...

Or maybe I'm not very good at making myself understood. I'm just... I'm upset at how much this is my fault, I guess. I was mad at my dad, I am mad at him, but you're right. He wouldn't hurt me on purpose. I feel all these things and no one seems to know, and I don't know how to fix it. Except...you I just talk to."

"I'm glad, Honey," he said. "Your dad does care about you though. He knew I wouldn't get rid of you." He slid his hand down her arm. "I was never going to throw you out on the street or take your job away."

He was callous sometimes, and he knew that. His life had made him that way. But he'd never do anything to intentionally hurt Honey.

"But working for you isn't exactly the same as having a real career, is it? It's not the same as what I thought I was working toward. I guess that I somehow managed to never really... That he never considered it... I don't know. I just feel so desperately like maybe no one's ever known me, and maybe I don't show who I am enough. I've always felt like I was really honest. About who I was and what I wanted, but you know, I hid wanting you the whole time. Really well. Maybe I'm just hiding. Maybe it's a whole lot of hiding."

"Hey," he said. "We're all hiding. The fact of the matter is… We've been almost like family this whole time."

She wrinkled her nose. "Gross."

"Well, it's true. And for family you put on a little bit of a performance. Because there's parts of yourself that you gotta keep quiet. It's just…what you do. It's just how you navigate things. At least… That's my experience of family. I never wanted my mom to know how difficult it was for me when she was sick. So I hid that. Because I had to be strong."

He wanted to talk to her, and he didn't much ever want to talk to anyone. But maybe it was what she'd said. About being misunderstood. Maybe that was why. Maybe he wanted to find ways they could understand each other.

She nodded. "Maybe that's it. I'm so used

to hiding what I want, because I wanted a lot of things that my dad couldn't give me. And I never wanted to make him sad. So I just… I kind of bump along and pretend everything is great. Even when it isn't."

"It is not too late," he said. "Obviously, there's no question of you going to see Donavan now."

"I took a job from him, Jericho. He needs at least time to find a replacement."

"You aren't touching him."

She looked shocked. "No, of course I wouldn't."

He didn't have the right to make that statement, not when they were supposed to just be…for the blizzard. But still. He couldn't stand the thought. It made him see red.

"I'm willing to sell you part of the winery."

And hell, there were layers of complications now. But this… This thing between them, it was only for the blizzard. It was only for the blizzard.

"You will?"

"Yeah," he said.

Because somewhere along the way the reason that he had wanted the winery, that desperate desire to claim his place in the valley, in the family... It had faded a little bit. Because he could see now that Honey wanted the same thing. And he didn't want to take it from her.

He would have, before this. Because what he wanted had felt more important, but it just didn't anymore.

"I'd like that. I mean, I have money. From the sale. We're just kind of passing it back and forth."

"You can make payments on a bigger part of the winery, if you want. Because otherwise you're only getting a fifth."

"I'll consider it. I'll buy a fifth, and then we'll see. If I want to pursue a bigger share, I will after that."

"That sounds a good plan."

"Can we get the Christmas tree now?"

"Yes," he said. "Bundle up. We'll go get a Christmas tree now."

* * *

By the time they got out of the tub and dressed, twilight had fallen. This single day had felt like four days. And Honey felt a little bit like she was in a daze. But the good kind.

Being with him had been… Transformative. She felt transformed.

She wasn't going to tell him that, because his ego was healthy enough without her stoking the flames, but it was true.

They didn't have to go far into the woods to find a decent tree, and Jericho chopped it down, then slung it over his shoulder to carry back. As he walked, icy little droplets fell from the tree and hit Honey in the face, but she didn't mind. She felt…renewed.

She was going to be able to buy a piece of the winery. She and Jericho were…

Something twisted in her stomach. *Nothing, you're nothing.*

Right. Of course. They weren't anything. They were just… For the blizzard.

The snow had eased up, no longer falling in large fat flakes and piling up higher and higher. Still, it was so cold it wouldn't be going anywhere for a while.

Before they went back to the cabin, Jericho walked to the truck and confirmed that it was still blocked in.

She laughed as he shook the tree out when they got to the porch, and then leaned it up against the wall in the living room, because there was no tree stand.

Honey found string and some popcorn kernels, which she popped on the stovetop in a big Dutch oven, and the two of them worked at making popcorn strings by lantern light, which then led to a contest to see who could make the most innocuous household object into a tree decoration.

In the end, their monstrous masterpiece included several ceramic figurines, a tinfoil star up on the very top and, possibly silliest of all, some perfume bottles hung from the branches by string, which ended up twinkling merrily in the lantern light and giving the entire thing a cheerfully strange effect.

"Without a doubt, the weirdest ass Christmas tree I have ever seen," Jericho said, taking a step back and putting his arm around her. The casual touch was so strange. How odd to have gone from existing in a space where it felt like there was a wall between them physically, to this moment, where they had now bathed together, and he was touching her like she was his...

She wasn't anything. She was just Honey.

She looked up at him, at his sculpted face, the firelight illuminating his brown skin. His dark eyes glittered there, his square jaw rough with black stubble, his lips... Well, now she knew what they tasted like. And what they felt like when they tasted her.

How could she ever go back to a time when she didn't know that? Where he wasn't hers anymore? To touch and do with as she pleased. How could she ever bear it?

You've borne a lot of things. You'll just have to bear this too.

She had more than she had when she'd first set out on this trip. She lost her virginity and she secured a job. It just wasn't what she'd been planning.

It was better.

She'd gotten what she wanted.

She wanted him physically, and nothing more.

And if the thought of that made her ache now… That was her own problem. It certainly wasn't his.

"It is indeed. But it's nice."

They lit a fire in the hearth there, and Jericho brought furs down from upstairs and spread them over the floor while Honey gathered together some cheeses, cured meats and crackers for a cheese board. There was even a glass of wine, and all up, the entire thing felt nearly sophisticated.

"I didn't imagine that being off-grid could be so glamorous."

"Helped very much by the fact that the generator runs some indoor plumbing," he pointed out.

"Well. There is that." She wrinkled her nose.

"Not much glamour to be had with an out-house."

"No indeed."

They settled into each other, into the moment. The furs soft and warm, the fire crackling in the hearth. It felt safe, right. She felt safe. To say what she needed to. To feel what she needed to.

The thought made her heart feel pierced, because her emotions had felt too big and wrong from the time she was a girl.

From back when her father had been so upset with her grief, and she had nearly drowned in it. And she'd learned to put it away because she'd had to.

"I never knew what to do about you," she said, her chest feeling tender. She shouldn't talk about this. Except, maybe it would help. Maybe it would explain things. Because she wasn't foolish enough to believe that she had a future with Jericho, and she never had been. It was just that... She knew him. And there was something about desiring him that had felt both dangerous and safe at the same time.

And maybe that was it. Maybe that was all it was. Because she hadn't had a mother to talk to her about those things...

"You were this...teenage boy that came into the house and you weren't my brother. And you made me feel all kinds of things and they were scary. I've never really had anyone I could talk to about this. Some casual friends at school when I was kind of on the outskirts of a couple of different groups. But I never really felt like I could share with them. I never really wanted to. It felt too... Precarious, I guess. I didn't know how I was going to explain to the girls in my class that I was more interested in a boy in his twenties than a boy my age. And I didn't really want to... I don't know. Maybe it's just that you've always felt safe."

"Safe?" he questioned, lifting his brows.

"You know. Not in a beige kind of way, but in a... I've always had a lot of feelings, and I've always been around men. And the way that men do feelings. And so I've always had to be really careful... Or I felt like I did.

Because I wanted to fit in and I wanted to be understood, but at the same time I didn't want my brothers or my dad to think that I was dramatic. And I didn't… I dunno, maybe keeping my sexual attraction type feelings down to somebody like you was… Because I could talk to you, always. Even with all of that. Because our relationship has always been… Sure, we fight and things like that, but it's always been important. And kinda special. And…"

"You've been lonely for a long time, haven't you?"

The words were far too incisive, and they hit Honey right where she lived.

"Yeah," she said. "I guess so."

"Well, we can talk."

"We've always been able to talk," she said. "I mean, that's what I'm saying."

"You did not tell me about the way you felt about the winery."

"Yes, I did. I just waited too long to do it. But you were still the first person that I told."

He shook his head. "Honey, you should've talked to me sooner."

"And what would you have said?"

He looked at her, long and hard. "That I was buying it. And you were out of luck."

"Yeah, I thought so."

"I feel differently about it now though."

"Oh please don't… Please don't be trading my virginity for a fifth of the winery."

He recoiled. "No," he said. "That's not it. It's talking to you. It's talking to you and understanding where you're coming from. What you want. It's actually listening. Which, I'm embarrassed to say, hasn't always been my strong point."

"Well, mine either. Which you know."

"Here we are. Listening."

She looked up at him, and her happiness suddenly felt so big that it threatened to overflow, and with that came a sense of wonder so big it threatened to burst from her mouth in the form of a song or a laugh or… Declarations that she wouldn't even really mean.

She didn't know if it was the wine making her a little bit tipsy or if it was just…him.

"This is the Maxfield label," she said. She shook her head. "So basic."

"The wine or the fact that they have it?"

"Regrettably, the wine is complex and lovely," she said.

"It is," Jericho said. "Not like my wine. Our wine." He shook his head. "This is some surreal stuff."

"What is?"

"I guess it's the same moment that you had up in the tub earlier. Us. Sitting here together. Drinking wine. I own a winery. Same as I don't know how I got from that boy to here."

"I do," she said. "You worked hard. I mean, you more than worked hard. You worked like there was a demon on your back."

"Yeah. I guess I did."

"And this is what you've earned. You know, less my fifth."

"True."

And suddenly, this wasn't enough. The joy that she had felt a moment ago was still there, but it had taken on a strange, sharp sensation. It made her feel like she was suffocating. Like she couldn't breathe.

There was a desperation with it. A hunger. And she didn't know how to satisfy it. Because it wasn't enough just to sit here with him. Wasn't enough just to talk to him. Suddenly, they weren't close enough. And much like what he'd said just a moment ago, she couldn't reconcile where they were right now with where they had been two days ago. The Honey and Jericho that had walked through the snow to this cabin were not the same two people that sat here now.

Or maybe they were. And that was the strangest part. That the transformation was so real. That it had actually just reshaped everything that she had believed about him, about herself. About her feelings. Or perhaps it had simply exposed what was already there. He had wanted her before. And she wanted him. It was just that they hadn't been able to be honest enough about it because their worries about what other people might think got in the way.

And there was none of that here.

This was like a snow globe, its own separate world with a beautiful glass dome that kept the bad parts away. Their trauma, their pasts. All the people they might disappoint, the future, and what they could or couldn't have in it. All of that. It was as if only they and this moment truly existed. Encircled by snow and magic and firelight. By an improbable Christmas tree and an improbable desire. Because outside of the space they were both…too them to ever make something work. That was just a fact. But here… Here it all seemed possible. And she wanted to seize hold of it. Wanted to grab it and hold it to her chest, claim it for herself, only for herself.

She felt wild with it. Selfish. And utterly and completely at peace with it.

Because he was hers. And this moment was hers.

And she wanted it to be naked.

She wanted him skin to skin. She wanted him inside of her.

She wrapped her arms around his neck and kissed him then. The flavor of the wine lingering on his lips, and the desperation of her desire creating a palpable need that drove her. Made her feel wild.

She clung to him, and she didn't know if she wanted him to feel what was inside of her, or if she never wanted him to know. If she didn't even want him to get a peek at the profound, forever changing sensations that were rolling through her. Her desire was so deep. So raw and real that it touched places in her own soul that she had never seen before, and the idea of sharing it was terrifying. So all she did was kiss him. All she did was kiss him, because it was all that could be done. Because everything else felt uncertain. Because she didn't even know what she wanted. Because she didn't have names for the feelings that ebbed and flowed and grew and snaked themselves around her like vines or glitter, magic or a curse, she didn't know.

She took her shirt off and cast it to the side, then pushed her hand beneath the waist of his. His body was solid, hard and well muscled, and her heart nearly leaped out of her chest when her fingertips grazed over his abs.

Because she had spent a lot of years fantasizing about this. About him, and emotion aside, there was just so much pent-up desire there.

No. There was no emotion aside, there never could be. And that had been her biggest mistake. Thinking that desire and emotion did not have to exist together. Thinking that she could simply ignore emotion. That she did not have to take it on board. Believing that she could have sex and go back to seeing him as she had done before, or maybe even with her attraction to him neatly removed, having been explored.

No. Instead, everything had gotten tangled together, and there was no going back to seeing him any other way besides this. Because it wasn't separate.

This need inside of her, the ache in her

chest, the man that he was. It wasn't separate. And it never could be.

She had been a fool for thinking so. For thinking that common sense and bird field guides and a hard limit on time could fix this thing. Could help them make sense of it and be sensible with it.

But there was no sense to be found here. It was only need.

It was only this.

But she tried to focus on the feel of him beneath her hands, tried to focus on his body, because at least while that overwhelmed, it was not as sharp as the rest.

She pushed his shirt up and off, moving her hands over his chest, down his stomach and back up again. Then she wrapped her arms around his neck and kissed him. Ran her hands over his short hair, down his muscled back as she tasted him. As she angled her head and took a deep breath, meeting the thrust of his tongue with enthusiasm.

He had taken her bra off and she hadn't

even noticed, not until one large hand came up to palm her naked breasts.

She shivered.

And she arched into him, wanting more. Craving more.

She found herself laid back against the soft furs, and he was over her, and she loved the feel of his body against hers. Luxuriating in it as he removed the rest of their clothes. And then suddenly, she got that feeling of being overwhelmed again. Of deep need that demolished her sanity. All the energy building inside of her propelled her forward, and she sat up, pressing her hands against his shoulders and pushing him back.

She moved so that she was over him, leaning over and kissing him hard, her heart hammering, threatening to beat right outside her chest. She ached between her legs. Felt hollow with her need for him. She reached over for his jeans and happily found his wallet and a condom inside.

She tore it open, then with shaking and uncertain fingers, wrapped her hand around the base of his arousal as she rolled the protection over him with deep concentration.

Then she positioned herself over his body, taking him in slowly, a moan of satisfaction rising in her throat as she did.

"Jericho," she whispered.

His hands came up and gripped her hips, his hold bruising, but she loved it.

She began to ride him. Establishing a rhythm that pleased them both, watching as the cords in his neck went tight with his need for her. She shivered. And nearly came right then, just from watching his pleasure.

From watching the effect that she had on him. He arched up into her, thrusting up, changing the tempo, the pace and the strength of it. She bowed over, grabbing hold of his face and kissing him on the mouth, shattering as her orgasm overtook her, wave after wave of pleasure that blended into his as he shouted his release, the two of them shaking and trembling in the aftermath.

Then he gathered her close, swept the

cheese platter to the side and wrapped them up in the furs.

She reached out and grabbed a cracker, chewing on the end as he held her close.

Because hopefully focusing on that would keep the tears at bay. Would keep her from dissolving completely.

How could they ever go back?

There was no going back, that much she knew. But maybe they could go forward and find a new shape. A new evolution. That was what this was, after all. A different sort of shape than what they'd been before. So no, they would never be able to be the exact thing they had been previously. But maybe they could find what Honey and Jericho after sex looked like. After baths and cheese platters and sharing secrets.

They had to. There was no other choice. She owned part of the winery now.

She had what she wanted.

Yet she felt hollow. A winery and a saltine cracker were not going to fix that.

Ten

When Jericho woke up the next morning, he could see that the sky was clear outside the window.

He was lying on the floor wrapped up in fur and Honey, still feeling the aftereffects of the night before. But he was going to have to check the weather.

He got up and put his pants on, then went out for his coat. He did his best to get out of the house without disturbing Honey. Outside it was completely quiet. Still. The sun was shining now, making it look like diamonds had been scattered across the surface of the undisturbed snow. The only dents had been made by their footprints last night when they went to get the Christmas tree.

It was bright today, and likely it would bring a little bit of snowmelt along with it.

It was Christmas Eve. He wondered if that meant there would be people coming to plow the roads or not.

He hiked out to the road, and there was a snowplow. There were also a few ODOT workers standing around.

"Hey," Jericho said to the first man, who was wearing a heavy coat and a bright yellow vest. "This is my truck," he said. "What are the odds that he gets out today?"

"We'll have this cleared within a couple of hours," the guy said.

"Thanks. It doesn't start well. Would I be able to get a tow truck out here you think?"

"Everything is eased up so much, and we're expecting highs to hit the fifties today. So this should be your window."

"Thanks," Jericho said.

He hiked back over to the house, where Honey was just beginning to stir.

"Looks like we'll be leaving today," he said.

She looked… Well, she looked stricken. But she didn't say anything. They started the task of putting everything in the house back the way they'd found it.

Jericho wrote a note with his contact information, asking that the owners tabulate the cost of what they had used and send him a bill. Plus charge whatever occupancy fees they normally did.

They looked at the tree.

"I guess we have to take it down. And put everything back."

It was a lot less festive than putting it up had been.

But they had everything restored to its rightful place, and he walked back up to the road to find his truck had had the snow cleared out from around it.

They could go.

"You ready?"

She nodded slowly. "Jericho… I'm not going to Lake Oswego."

He froze.

"All right."

"I think you already knew that. You know, what with the offer of the winery and all."

"Well, yeah."

"But I would like to go to Christmas with you. For… For the Daltons and all that."

"Oh," he said. "Well, that's…good of you."

"It's not good of me. I want to go with you. This is going to be super… Super weird for you. Wouldn't you like to have a friend with you?"

"Yeah," he said. "A friend."

Honey was his friend. But the word felt limp in comparison to what they'd been here. Where they were snowbound and hot as fire anyway. Where they'd talked and made love and decorated the first Christmas tree he'd touched since he was sixteen.

A friend.

He supposed that's how it would have to be

explained to Jackson and Creed when it came up. Because it would come up.

As soon as they hit civilization, their phones were going to go crazy.

They'd been out of communication for nearly three days.

It suddenly felt like longer, and a lot less time all at once. It would be like walking through a veil. Where everything changed when they got back to civilization. And she wanted to go with him to see the Daltons.

He helped her carry her bags through the woods, back to the truck.

And when they climbed inside, it all felt a little bit too modern.

She laughed. "I'm not going to know what to do when a heater just comes on."

It was funny the way her mind tracked with his. For a minute, he wondered if the engine would even turn over, but it did. And it was a strange little string of miracles, if he was honest. From the vacation rental down to this.

I mean, it made him question why they had to be caught in the snowstorm in the first place, but everything that had happened since had a strange sort of charmed feeling to it. He would've called it fate if he believed in things like that.

Hell, he couldn't actually fathom that fate had led him to cozy up with his friends' sister for a few nights of pleasure. Hell, one night. Hadn't been enough. But it was done now. It was done now because it had to be.

The heater got going and the only sound was the air, the tires on the newly plowed and graveled road and the engine.

They had talked easily at the vacation rental, but neither of them seemed to know what to say now.

Now it seemed like…

"When do you think we will have service?" She was looking down at her phone.

"I have no idea. I didn't know there was as big of a dead zone out here as there is."

"Oh," she said, tapping her fingers on the door.

"Right."

"So."

They said nothing for another whole minute.

"What if… What if we kept on doing it. You know, just while we're away," she continued.

He looked over at her, and she was staring fixedly out the window.

"Are you looking for birds out there?"

"No," she said, looking back at him. "I just… Yeah I… Maybe we should… Keep doing it. Yeah. Don't you think that would be fun?"

"Fun," he echoed.

"Yeah. Fun. Real fun."

"Look," she said. "If you don't want to do it."

"No. I don't want to make a bigger mess out of this than we already have. At least before we came to the cabin, we would fight when we were sitting together in a car. Now we can barely speak a sentence to each other."

"That's a very coherent sentence," she said.

"Thanks," he said.

"I mean… I just can't see being at the Dalton place and not doing it."

"We should have just gone back."

"No. Let's do this." She slapped her hand on her thighs. "We're survivalists."

"Right."

"We are. And… I still feel bad that I never really… That I didn't realize what a big thing it was. You finding out that Hank never knew about you. I didn't really think about it. And I'm embarrassed. And if I can help you through it any way, I want to do that."

"And you want to get laid," he said, unable to keep the smile from curving his lips, even though mostly the entire topic wasn't that amusing to him.

"Well, I'm not dead below the waist. Or anywhere, for that matter. So all right. Maybe I want more."

More.

More.

He tried not to let that word resonate too much inside of him. Because she meant more sex, and more sex was all it could be. More sex wasn't what it should be, but still.

More.

More people in his family. And with that, just more complication in general. Yeah, initially he thought he'd show up and flaunt his wealth. His success. And now he was…bringing a girl home to meet his folks. Well, his dad anyway. His father.

Tammy Dalton was not his mother. Tammy Dalton was the reason his life had gone the way that it had.

He wasn't going to let himself get too bitter about it. Mostly because, even though what Tammy had done was wrong, Hank had committed the first wrong, and he didn't know if a person was responsible for being perfect in response to something like that.

Still. She was just the woman who had paid his mother off and made her go away. Who had lied to her husband about the extent of his misdeeds for all those years.

"Looks like we'll make it in time for Christmas Eve dinner."

The rest… He wasn't going to think about.

It took another couple of hours to get up to the compound, and by the time they did, they had cell service. He could call and let the Daltons know he was coming, but the idea of speaking to them on the phone felt...wrong somehow. He didn't want to answer questions about where he'd been. He had directions to the cabin that was his for the next couple of days, and he went straight there.

"I guess dinner is kind of a formal affair," he said. "I don't think your lingerie is going to cut it."

"Oh, I have something," she said. "I was prepared for the fanciness of Lake Oswego."

She was a dark horse, was Honey Cooper. And that was for certain.

The cabin itself was small but luxurious compared to where they'd just been. It had all the modern amenities, hypermodern even. A steam shower, not a wood sauna, and towel warmers and lights. There were lights. He may have stopped and flipped the switch off and on a couple of times.

"What are you doing?" Honey asked.

"Aren't you amazed by the electricity?"

"I'm not that far gone," she said.

"Have you looked at your phone yet?"

"No," she said, wincing. "I was expecting to get chewed out by my dad and my brothers for my disappearing act, and that was when I just thought I was going up to Lake Oswego and would be able to contact them that same day. Though I guess… At least… At least I'm not moving."

"Should we get dressed for dinner?" he asked.

"Yeah," she replied.

She disappeared off into one of the other bedrooms, which he thought was interesting, considering she was the one who had suggested they keep things up. Not that he was complaining. And he couldn't stop himself from imagining her getting undressed now. Peeling her clothes off, revealing her beautiful body.

He gritted his teeth, then went to the other bedroom with his suitcase and took out the suit that he brought for the occasion. He dressed and put a black cowboy hat on his head. And he figured he probably looked more rodeo royalty than Hank Dalton did on a good day.

He went out to the living room, and Honey still hadn't appeared. He checked his watch, waiting.

And then she emerged, wearing a figure-hugging red dress, her hair spilling over her shoulders in a curled cascade. He couldn't remember ever seeing Honey in makeup, the effect dramatically highlighting all the things about her that were already beautiful.

"Damn," he said.

"Do I meet with your approval?"

"Hell yeah," he responded.

She smiled.

"Is that why you hid from me?"

"Well, yes. I wanted there to be a little bit of a surprise."

"You are a surprise, Honey. Every day. In a thousand different ways."

He linked arms with her, and led her out of the cabin. It was dark out, but it was easy to navigate their way from there to the main house, which he knew Hank and the rest of the family were in.

He had been told to just come in when they arrived, so he did. Pushing the door open and revealing a glittering Christmas scene. A huge tree that had to be eighteen feet high at least, stretching up to the top ceiling beam, casting a warm glow over the room. There were garlands and big velvet bows. On the big mezzanine floor that overlooked the living area. No one was here, but he could hear voices coming from what he assumed might be the dining room.

He took Honey's hand. Without even thinking.

They walked down the short hallway and went to the left, and there it was. There everyone was. The table was massive, laden with food, huge candelabras in the center, along with tiered trays of meats and desserts. It was the gaudiest, tackiest thing he'd ever seen this side of the *Harry Potter* movies, and it was incredible.

And around that table was… Everyone.

Hank at the head, wearing a white cowboy hat and suit, along with a bolero tie. Tammy at the foot of the table with big hair and a big smile.

And filling in the middle part… His half siblings and their spouses. Everyone went around the table for a quick intro.

West, who he'd met, and his wife, Pansy. Gabe, Jacob and Caleb, with their wives and kids. Logan and his wife, and McKenna, the lone sister, and her husband.

He knew who they all were, but he hadn't… Had never really thought that he'd be part of the family. Not ever.

But here they were. And here he was.

At a crowded table, and he had the strangest ache at the center of his chest that he ever felt.

"Jericho," Hank said. "We thought you decided not to come."

"I got waylaid by the snowstorm. We had to wait it out in a cabin on the way here."

"No shit," Hank said, laughing. "That must be quite a story. Pull up a chair. Who is this?"

"Honey," he said. "She's a…a family friend."

"He's not calling me *honey*," she said. "My first name is Honey."

Hank laughed at that too. "I love it."

"My parents are…were…are eccentric," Honey said.

"Eccentric," he said. "I like it. I can definitely understand eccentric."

It was Tammy, though, who stood.

There was a strange, soft note in her eyes, and Jericho couldn't say that he liked it much.

It was too much like pity. Or sorrow.

"I'm glad you could come," she said, walking forward and reaching her hand out.

It was Honey took it. "Thank you," she said.

And he realized that Honey was protecting him. That she had sensed his hesitance and put herself right in Tammy's path.

"Have a seat," Hank said. "The food's getting cold."

"Thanks," Jericho said.

They added another chair for Honey quickly, and they sat down beside each other. Honey made quick work of putting her plate together, then jumped right into the chatting.

And he had never been more grateful to have someone he knew at his side than he was right at this moment.

Because she was covering the awkwardness with ease, and he had never really thought that Honey was the kind of person who would do that.

"So what is it you do?" This question came from Grant, who he supposed was his half brother-in-law.

"I own Cowboy Wines."

"Are you familiar with Grassroots Winery?"

"Yeah," Jericho said.

"That's my sister-in-law's. She's great. If you like to do any kind of collaborating, you should have a chat with Lindy."

The family connections just kept growing. But he supposed that was the nature of something like this.

He wasn't clear on everyone's stories or circumstances, but as the evening wore on, he began to get filled in with bits and pieces of conversation. Grant and McKenna had met and married several years ago when she had come to town looking for Hank. Grant had lost his wife several years before and had never really thought about getting married again.

West was an ex-convict, and as opposite to his wife—a good girl police officer—as it was possible to get.

But they seemed completely crazy about each other.

Gabe Dalton's wife was a total horse girl, and had plenty in common with Honey, who took up easy chatting with her over dessert.

Jacob and Caleb were married to teachers—who taught at the school for troubled kids that was apparently now on Dalton land. Logan and his wife were ranchers.

They were an interesting group, all with completely different stories. Though loss was something most of them had dealt with in one form or another. McKenna had been abandoned by her mother, while Logan's had died.

He felt an immediate kinship to him.

He vaguely remembered Logan from high

school, though they weren't in the same year. And he'd been too caught up in his own grief to think about a kid younger than him dealing with anything similar.

The fact was, tragedy was more commonplace than anybody really liked to think.

It made your aches and pains feel like garden-variety stuff, when it felt absolutely significant to you.

He wasn't sure if it made it worse or better. He had lived in a cloistered version of this experience for most of his life. What he wasn't used to was having casual conversations about things like this with people he didn't even really know all that well.

"So she's a friend?" West asked, looking at him pointedly, then over at Honey, who was chatting with Jamie and Rose.

"Yeah," he said. "Actually, my friends' sister…"

At that, Gabe and Logan laughed. They laughed.

"What?"

"Been there," Logan said.

"Married that," Gabe added.

"Well, I'm not getting married."

"Why not?" West asked. "I recommend the institution, actually, and I never did think that I would."

"Nice for you," Jericho said. "But…"

"Oh, have you had a hard life?" West asked.

"Too bad," Logan said.

"Are we talking about hard lives?" McKenna came over to them, hands on her hips. "I'd like to play. Who had ten homes in four years?"

"You win that game," West said. "I had way less. Well, not way less."

"But who has the most half siblings?"

"I wouldn't know," McKenna said. "Because I don't know my mom."

"I only have the one other half sibling that I know of." West looked at Jericho. "No relation to us. My mom's kid."

"Just you people," Gabe said.

"Same," Logan added.

"You all seem pretty…relaxed about this."

"No point getting wound up about it at this

point," Gabe said. "Now, that wasn't true back when it all first... Back when it all first happened."

"Yeah, it was not the best when I showed up," McKenna said. "Everyone was trying to put all the unpleasantness of the past behind them, and there I was, a big reminder of the way things had been before."

"No one blames you for that," Gabe said.

"I know you don't," McKenna said. "And I'm glad that I came here. If I hadn't... I wouldn't have all of you. Or Grant."

"I think you like Grant best," Logan said.

"I do," McKenna said. And that made her brothers laugh.

Her brothers. He supposed they were his brothers. And he was her brother.

Growing up an only child, that was a strange thing to wrap his head around. Sure, he had been brought into the Cooper family, but it wasn't quite the same. And he'd been sixteen when he had been.

Of course, he was thirty-four now.

"I think you like her," McKenna said.

"Well, you don't know me," Jericho answered.

"Oh good," McKenna said, smiling. "You have a chip on your shoulder. You really will fit in nicely. I was feral when I first came here."

"I'm not exactly feral," he said.

"But not exactly not," McKenna said.

All right, that was a fair enough characterization of him in the entire situation. But he wasn't going to let her know.

"Well, it's getting late."

"You have to make sure you get back here bright and early," McKenna said. "They take the present opening very seriously."

"We do," said his brother Caleb's wife, Ellie, holding a baby and hanging on to her seven-year-old, who was looking terribly sleepy.

"Yeah, and Amelia isn't going to wait," Caleb said, indicating the child.

He stood up, and Honey stiffened. She wasn't even looking at him, but she seemed to sense his move to leave. He couldn't begin to figure out how she was so in tune with him. It was just the strangest thing. The way she seemed to know what he felt. The fact that she was here at all.

"I'm going to head back to the cabin," Honey said. "I need to call my dad. I'll see you in, like, ten minutes."

That surprised him. Because he thought that she had sensed his readiness to leave. But then she was scampering out, saying good-night to everybody, and Hank was looking at him. And he realized she had done that on purpose.

She was sensing things, but she wasn't on his team.

"Hey there, son," Hank said. "I wanted to have a talk with you."

"You don't have to do that."

"I don't have to do what?"

"Call me *son*."

"Maybe I don't have to. But I want to."

Maybe I don't want you to. But he didn't say that. Because he was here to see Hank,

230 RANCHER'S CHRISTMAS STORM

after all, so what was the point of being hostile. At least overtly.

Hank stood, and he followed him out of the room, back into the grand dining room, which was now empty. "Thank you for coming," he said. "I didn't think you would. But you know... Whether you believe it or not, I've known you were out there for a while. I just didn't know your name. And her last name made it tricky to track you down. I had never gotten your first name, and your mother, Letty Smith, it was a common name. And when I finally did find her... And I found out she was gone..."

"Yeah. She died when I was sixteen."

"I'm sorry. I didn't know."

"I know you didn't, Hank."

"You thought I did though. For your whole life, didn't you?"

"Yeah. But you know... It's good to have an enemy. Good to have a bad object that you can fight against. It's probably why I have been so successful." There he was, giving him credit for something that he had been bound and determined not to give him credit for. Even if he had said it as a joke, it was closer to acknowledging the role that Hank had played in his life than he wanted.

"Sure," Hank said. "I know a little something about that. I ran from my demons for a long time. And they took me to dark places. I wasn't a good husband to Tammy. And I failed a lot of other women as a result too. McKenna is working on teaching me about feminism."

"Is she?" Jericho asked, and that was truly the funniest thing he'd ever heard.

"Yeah," he said. "Because of the patriarchy and power imbalances and things, what I did was especially wrong. But at the time it just felt like… I didn't feel particularly powerful. I felt like a dumb kid that was out of control. I felt like a fool. Someone who didn't deserve any of the things that he had. Who was just trying to feel alive. But at some point, you have to feel more than alive, and you have to work at feeling more than good. What you have to do is learn to sit on your bad feelings. That's a hell of a thing."

"Yeah, I've had enough bad feelings to get me through for a long time."

"I'm not meaning to lecture you. I'm just… I'm glad that you're here, I hope that I'll see you past Christmas. I hope that you give this family thing a chance."

"Then that would give you a happy ending, wouldn't it? It would make all of it seem like it had a meaning? If you could get all of your wayward kids here and happy to be with you. Everybody forgiving everybody else and getting along. I guess that would go a long way in soothing your guilt."

Guilt.

He was more familiar with the concept than he'd like.

Especially in regards to Honey.

Not touching her. He couldn't feel guilty about that.

But because of all he could never give her.

"Sure," he said. "But you know, it's a lot of guilt, Jericho. Because McKenna was in foster care for all of her life. And Logan lost his mother. And you lost yours. And you boys were alone. McKenna was alone. There's a lot of guilt with that. It's not easy to live with."

"Well, we'll see what happens. But whatever happens, I'm not making the decision for the purpose of saving your soul. I enjoyed tonight. But I have a life. I have family." The Coopers, whom he was drastically betraying with his dalliance with Honey. But he wasn't going to think about that.

"I wouldn't ask you to," Hank said. "I wouldn't ask you to do anything for the purpose of appeasing me. But sure, the side effect is that it probably will. If that stops you then… Not much I can do about it."

"Sorry," Jericho said. "It's been a hell of a trip up here. It's been a hell of a few days. I don't know if I'm coming or going. But I'll be here for Christmas morning."

"Merry Christmas," Hank said. Then as Jericho turned to go, he added, "Son."

Hank was pushing. Jericho should be furious and yet…

He'd been a boy with no one. When he'd been sixteen and people had complained about annoying parents... He'd been nothing but jealous.

Something in him... Something in him wanted this and he couldn't deny it, even as the wounded part of him wanted to pull away from it.

Jericho turned. "You couldn't resist."

"I couldn't."

"You did it because I told you not to."

"Maybe. Look. I might've tried to better myself, but I'm still a no-good jackass. I just keep it managed now."

"Well, see that you do."

"Also, I'm going to have to build the bridge between us," Hank said, his voice full of gravity. "No matter how wide the valley is, I'm committed to it, Jericho, I promise you. But I'm the one that should have to work for it. I'm the one who messed up. I just hope you'll stick out waiting for me to get to the other side."

Jericho's throat went tight. "Yeah. Sure."

Which wasn't enough, but there were no other words.

He turned and walked down the long hall, out the front door, managing to slide by everybody without having to say a string of long messy good-nights.

He didn't think he could face that level of family.

Outside it was crisp and cold and the sky was clear, the stars twinkling above, the trees inky black with spots of white snow a shout in the dark.

He had a family back in that house. A family.

And a woman waiting for him at his cabin.

And suddenly, his life felt fuller than it ever had.

Eleven

"I'm okay, Dad," she said, pacing back and forth in the living room. It was a little bit dastardly that she had left Jericho to talk to Hank. She had realized at some point that Hank was itching to do it, and she knew that unless she did something like this, Jericho was going to come back to the cabin with her.

But, she needed to talk to her dad. He needed to talk to his.

"I wish you would've talked to me about leaving in the first place. By the time I found out you'd gone up north, you were already gone, and then I had no way of knowing that you were trapped in a snowstorm."

"Jericho found me," she said. "We found a vacation rental. We hunkered down there." And the less she said about it the better. "And then I decided to come up with him to support him while he met with his dad."

"You're not usually all that friendly with him."

"Well, he saved my life. I mean, really, if I hadn't been with him I don't know what would've happened. And I'm not moving. I changed my mind."

She'd left it all in her note. Well, nothing about her virginity of course.

"Really?" her dad said.

"Yeah. Really. I talked to Jericho, and he said that he's going to sell me a portion of the vineyard back."

"Did you... Did you want some of the vineyard?"

"Yes, Dad. I wanted it desperately. It's why I've been furious for the last few months."

"You've been furious?"

She'd been so honest with Jericho. And the walls she'd always felt existed between herself and the world felt thinner now. And she liked it that way.

So why not speak?

Why not now?

She'd been ready to leave. Which was so extreme in hindsight. More ready to run than have a conversation.

But being with him had changed her.

And this was her moment to live in that change.

"Yes. Furious. Absolutely incensed that you would do that to me. That you would sell the winery out from under me without talking to me first. It's why I decided to move away. But, Jericho saved me from the snowstorm, and we talked about my future."

There. Now Jericho sounded like a hero.

She heard female voices in the background. "Are you at the Maxfields'?"

"Yes," he said.

"Are you and…"

"I really do love her, Honey."

"Right. You love her and… I guess you're going to marry her and close this big strange circle of our families?"

"Well, that depends. She ended up getting so much of the winery. She's a very rich woman. I'm not sure that she's interested in getting hitched. We might just live in sin."

"Oh, for heaven's sake, Dad. I don't want to know that."

"You should be happy for me. I've been miserable for a long time."

"I am happy for you. Only if you can be happy for me too. And realize that for me the winery is happiness."

"Of course, Honey. I only want what's best for you. I'm sorry if I didn't see it. I just… I was never very good at having a daughter."

"I don't know, sometimes I wonder if I was any good at being one. I just wanted to be like the boys. But I'm not. They're outspoken and they know how to tell you what they want. And they do it without emotions. But I have feelings. A lot of them, and I just spent a lot of time shoving them down deep.

I didn't want to cause trouble. I know how much it upset you... The way I was at Mom's funeral."

It was a memory that lodged deep inside of her. One that she didn't like to talk about.

"It was an upsetting time."

"I just didn't want to upset you. Not again."

"I love you, Honey. You don't upset me. I think sometimes I just don't look at you and know immediately what you want."

She thought of Jackson and Creed and the different things they'd been through, and honestly, she didn't think her dad knew anymore what they wanted. Hell, they hadn't known what they wanted until they'd gotten with Wren and Cricket. So maybe that was just it. Maybe everybody was always learning, and they needed to do a better job of talking.

"I love you, Dad," she said. "I'll be home in a couple of days."

"Tell Jericho no funny business."

And then her dad laughed, as her heart shimmered down into her stomach. And she realized he thought it was a hilarious joke.

"I think I'll let him have his way with me," she said.

"You do that," her dad said.

"Merry Christmas," she said.

And then got off the phone, happy that the idea of Jericho touching her was just such a joke.

She frowned furiously, and was still frowning at the front door when it opened and Jericho came in.

"Hey," he said. "What's up?"

"I told my dad I was going to let you have your way with me, and he literally laughed."

"Oh, don't take offense to that," Jericho said, shrugging out of his jacket. And she couldn't help but admire the muscles in his body as he moved. In fact, she just went ahead and ogled him, because she was out of sorts, and she felt owed.

"Why should I not take offense?"

"Because it's to do with it being you and me. It's not you."

"Well, why do people think we're so incompatible?"

"Because we bicker."

"So what?"

"Well, we bicker quite a bit."

"Clearly unresolved sexual tension. Haven't they ever seen a romantic comedy?"

He crossed the room, wrapped his arm around her waist and drew her up against him. He gripped her chin between his thumb and forefinger, his dark eyes intense. "Honey, we are not a romantic comedy." And she could feel the evidence of his desire pressing against her body. And no. They were not a comedy. There was nothing funny about this.

"Okay," she said.

And what she meant was, *I trust you.* What she meant was, *you matter to me.*

And he seemed to know that, because he leaned in and kissed her on the lips.

"It's Christmas Eve," she said.

"It's Christmas Eve."

"Did you like Christmas when you were a kid?"

"No," he said, his voice hoarse. "I hated it. I always had to figure out ways to get Christmas decorations up. Get a tree. Get a meal from the local church, so that we had something nice, even though in the end my mom didn't want to eat. But somebody had to make Christmas happen. And she didn't have the energy to do it. So I always did. After she died, I just didn't do it. I mean, I would go be with your family, but I haven't put up a decoration in my own house... Ever."

"Jericho," she whispered. "I'm so sorry." Because for all that she had felt like she had to do something to hide her emotions, there had always been people there taking care of her. It might not have been perfect, but she wasn't alone. She might've had moments of loneliness, but that was different than being alone. It was different than being a child who was expected to be an adult. Different than being forced to be the one that brought the Christmas magic into the house when people should've been making it happen for you.

"You never believed in Santa Claus, did you?"

He shook his head. "No. Because I figured

I was about as good as a kid could be. So if I was going to magically get gifts… No. I didn't. I wanted to believe in Jesus though. Because that made me feel less alone. So that was about…the only point of Christmas as far as I could see. Well, and Christmas dinners made by church ladies."

"I'm so sorry."

"It's okay. I've made it okay."

But when he smiled, it didn't reach his eyes, and she wondered how she hadn't realized that before.

And she knew what it was like. To carry things that were absolutely not okay, but to also realize there was no point mourning what you should've had, because none of it was going to bring it back to you. But her heart ached for the little boy who had made sure there was Christmas for his mother. Who probably needed there to be Christmas so that she didn't feel quite like she was failing him so badly, but it had rebounded and turned into something he had to perform. And it made her feel so… So desperately sad.

And for the first time, she wanted to tell the story of what happened at her mother's funeral. She had never talked about it with anyone. Until she had mentioned it with her dad a few moments ago, they had never even brought it up to each other.

"I was so sad when my mother died," she said. "I couldn't stop crying. I thought I was going to die myself. I was gasping for air, gulping. It lasted…days, Jericho. Days. Then I stopped. And it was just sort of a horrible silence. But then at the funeral it all came back. And I just… I screamed. And I cried. My father was so distressed, he didn't know what to do with me. He was stoic, and the boys were stoic. And…"

"You were a little girl."

"I know," she said. "I was a little girl who really really missed her mother. And… My father found it so upsetting. He didn't know what to do with me. He told me to be quiet. And he told me to stop crying. He told me to wait outside the church until I could get my emotions together."

"Honey..."

"So I just sat there and I bit my tongue through the whole thing. And eventually, the pain did something to block out my sadness. The tears. I just tried after that. Every day. To be a little bit stronger. Because I realized that...on top of everything else my dad couldn't handle my sorrow."

"Dammit," Jericho said. He put his hand up to her cheek. "That's wrong."

"He was just trying his best. It's like Christmases that you have to throw yourself when you're a child. Yeah, it's sad. But... There's nothing you can do about it. We just got stronger. We just did the best we could."

"You don't have to hide yourself. Not now."

She could tell he hadn't meant to say it.

"You don't have to hide yourself either."

And then he was kissing her. When she thought they might both be consumed by it. By the flames of their desire. The fire of this need between them that could no longer be controlled. And she couldn't quite wrap her mind around this Jericho. Vulnerable, strong.

Sexy. So much more than the man she'd always seen. The man she'd wanted, but the man she hadn't really known.

He was… He was brilliant and wonderful and everything. And so strong, so amazingly resilient, having been through so much.

And she wondered how she had ever believed that it was a crush. How she had ever thought that all that they were could be reduced to something so basic, so…juvenile.

Because it was easier. Because it was then. But all it had taken was a few honest conversations, and it was different. She was different. And she saw the ways that he was different.

And that they were the same. All the ways that he was able to fill the gaps in who she was, and who they both were. And the way that she was able to do the same for him.

And she kissed him. Because she wanted him. Because he was the man she'd always known, and this man she had gotten to know over the past few days. Because he was her brothers' friend, but most importantly he was

her friend. Because they were business part-
ners and they had known each other half their
lives. Because... Well, quite simply because
she loved him.

And it was a truth that rang out as clear and
lovely inside of her as anything ever could
have. It was a truth that reverberated across
her soul. She loved him. And she was in love
with him. It was every layer, every piece of
all the ways she'd seen him bonded together
in one strong undeniable feeling. Because
she saw the truth of who he was now. The
whole of him. All of him. And because of
that she saw the whole of herself, as well.
The woman that she was. The woman that
she wanted to be.

The ways that she had been hurt and the
way that she had overcome. And the way that
she wanted him. The way that she loved him.
She was no longer protecting herself, because
that was what it had been. Telling herself it
was a crush. Pushing herself to find a way
to get over him. To be with someone else,

because of course being with someone else would've been easy. The easiest thing.

Because Donovan might have taken her clothes off her, but he would never have stripped her bare. And Jericho had brought her down to the truth of who she was.

Jericho was… He was the only man for her. The only one that she could ever love. And she did. She had told him… Oh, foolish her, she had told him that she didn't expect them to get married or be in a relationship, or be anything. And she had been wrong. She had lied, even though she hadn't meant to. Because she had hoped. She had always hoped. And in a life that had given her so few reasons to hope, this one last bit of light had existed in the very corner of her soul, reserved for him, reserved for this. For all that she wished they could be.

And she kissed him with that truth. All of it, resonating inside of her.

And when he picked her up and carried her to his bedroom, she didn't make any comments about his carrying her, didn't try to defuse the tension with a joke. No. She was there. Completely. Doing nothing to block out the intensity of her need for him. The intensity of their desire for one another.

It was raw and real, and she would do nothing to make it less.

She wrenched his black tie loose, slid it through the collar of his shirt and cast it down to the floor. Pushed his jacket from his shoulders and unbuttoned his white shirt, revealing a wedge of tan skin. He was so beautiful.

Utterly brilliant in all of his glory. Whether he was in a T-shirt and jeans or a suit. Naked, which was how she preferred him most of all.

She stripped him bare, like it might give her access to the deepest parts of him. Like it might give her a part of his soul, that part of him that she so desperately craved.

She stripped him bare, as if she was dependent upon it.

And then he was naked before her, his eyes shining with the light of intensity that ignited her from within.

She reached behind her back and grabbed

the zipper pull on her dress and let it fall free, let it pool at her feet. She was wearing some of the lingerie. Lacy and white, bridal, it could be said.

And the way that he looked at her, as if he wanted to devour her, satisfied her. Made her feel utterly and completely captured. By a look. By the promise of his touch. By the desperate hope of his love.

And when they were finally joined together, laid out on the bed, she wrapped her arms around his neck and kissed him. Poured out every ounce of her love—her love because she would name it now—into that kiss.

She had been afraid before, of all the things rising up inside of her.

Because she had been afraid of her feelings for so long. For too long.

But they were here, and they were big. Bigger than she was. Maybe bigger than the both of them. Maybe they would consume her. Maybe they would swallow them both. Maybe it would leave her with desperate, sad scars, but she could no longer live a life where she denied all that she was for the sake of safety. For the sake of making everyone else comfortable.

She had to do this. She had to step into who she was. Into who she hoped to be. Because the only reason she had ever been unhappy was because of her own self. Because she had kept too many things to herself. Whether it be her feelings about the winery or her feelings about Jericho. The way that she felt disconnected from her family sometimes... She was the one that had chosen to keep them locked down deep, and it might've been for other people, but no one had ever outright asked for it. And even if they had... Why did she have to give everybody what they wanted?

Couldn't she have something for herself?

Perhaps this was growth, and other people needed to grow right along with her.

Perhaps, she wasn't the one who was broken.

"I love you," she whispered.

And then they both went over the edge together.

* * *

Jericho was shaking. The aftermath of the pleasure he just experienced roared in his blood, in his head, along with Honey's words.

"I love you."

His chest felt like it had been rent. With sharp claws and sweet words, and everything Honey.

"Honey… Don't do this."

"Don't do what?"

She rolled away from him, all soft and naked, and he wanted to bring her back into his arms, because what he wanted to do was hold her all night. He didn't want her to do this. They were supposed to have this thing until they all went back to their real lives. It was still Christmas. He was still supposed to get to have this.

"Don't do what?" she repeated.

"Don't make this into something that it isn't supposed to be," he said.

"Who gets to say?"

"We already said."

"Yeah. Things change. Life is not fair. You

and I both know that. Why are you acting like just because we decided on something doesn't mean we can't change our minds."

"Because I can't," he said, looking at her earnest face, feeling his heart beating so hard he thought it might tear through his chest and land bloody on the bed in front of them.

"So I was just supposed to keep my feelings to myself again. How is that any different than what my dad wanted me to do when he made me sit outside of my mother's funeral."

"Because that was real," he said. "Those feelings were real. But this… This is just you having your first sex partner."

He felt like he was standing on the edge of a dark, endless well and all that was down there was…grief.

All-consuming, terrifying.

It was the only path love led to.

It took and took and took, until in the end, love took itself away too and you were cut off at the knees.

He couldn't.

He *couldn't*.

"Don't do that to me," she said. "Do not be condescending to me. I am not a child. I am a woman. And what life has thrown at you it's thrown at me too. I know what it's like to lose somebody that I love. I know it. Deep in my soul. To miss someone all the time that you can never see again. To feel so isolated in your grief, even though there are people around you who should understand. To feel the way that it burns when you just need this person who's gone forever. I know. I had to grow up early too. I get it."

"You didn't have to throw your own Christmas."

"No. I'm not saying I had every hardship you did, but I am not a baby. Don't treat me like one. Don't you dare."

"I'm not treating you like a baby, but I am treating you like what you are. A woman with vastly less experience than I have. And I think you want to listen to me when I tell you that you're probably just putting too much weight on this."

"As if you don't put any weight on it," she

said. "As if it doesn't matter to you at all that we had sex."

"I'm not saying it doesn't matter."

"What are you saying then?"

"I don't want love. Not yours, not anyone's. It is too much work, Honey. And I am not worth the struggle."

"That isn't true."

"Fine then. I don't think it's worth the struggle. I don't want it. I don't want to do it. I don't want your love. I don't want to love you back. I just wanted to fuck. That's it. I think you're hot—I have for a long time. You told me you were going to go give your virginity to some other guy, and it pissed me off. Because I'm a guy. But that's it. It's the beginning and end of the story."

Tears were running down her face, and he felt like… He was the worst. He was the absolute worst person. He hated himself just then. But all he could think of was that horrific, weighted feeling when Christmas rolled around. When he had to do everything and make things merry and bright and pretend that he wasn't living in some damned horror show in his heart, where he knew that the end of his mother's life was coming, and he knew that he was facing a future by himself, and it was just spinning out slowly and terribly, and he was putting on a grim performance in the meantime. He couldn't stand it. He simply couldn't stand it. The expectation. The certain feeling that no matter what, no matter how much he loved, no matter what he did, he was hurtling toward an inevitable end, something that would never be fixed or satisfied.

And he couldn't. He just couldn't.

"Honey… No. We can't do this."

And her face crumpled. And he felt like an absolute ass.

But there was nothing he could do about it. Sitting there, lost in every bad feeling that he'd ever had in his life, every grief that he never contended with, he simply couldn't do it. She got up, and she walked out of the room.

And it took him a few minutes to realize

that she wasn't just leaving the room. She was leaving.

A car pulled up to get her some fifteen minutes later. And then she was gone. And he was left. Crushed beneath the weight of damn near everything.

He looked outside the cabin window and he saw the Christmas tree shining through the window of the main house. And he nearly choked.

Merry Christmas.

This was what Christmas was all about. At least what it always had been for him.

Being given a taste of something, something brilliant and beautiful and hopeful, the light of the damned world.

Knowing that darkness hovered around the edges, knowing that this feeling could never really be his.

That was what Christmas was to him.

Apparently, it was what it always would be.

Twelve

Honey didn't collapse until she got home and climbed into bed.

Then she wept like she was dying.

It was two o'clock in the morning by the time she got back to Gold Valley, and she was a whole disaster mess.

She cried and cried, and then slept for about two hours before climbing out of bed and putting on clothes to go to the Maxfields. Because even though she didn't want to see anybody, she figured she had to go do it. Because it was Christmas.

But she felt devastated. Horrendously.

And she hoped that she could pull it together for the celebrations.

But what if you didn't? What if you let them know that you were hurt?

The idea made her shiver slightly.

But still, she got dressed and went into the house.

"Honey," Emerson said. "We weren't expecting you."

"I'm here," she said, looking around the Tuscan-style villa, feeling as hideously out of place there as she always did.

The Maxfields were fancy. Fancy fancy, and she had never really felt comfortable with it.

But why? She supposed it was because she was afraid of what they might think. That she might not blend.

That she might stand out.

Well, who cared.

She wasn't fancy.

Neither was Cricket.

And all the worries that she had about connecting with Cricket were based around what

Cricket might think too. Because she was just so… She was so consumed by that. By making everybody comfortable, and not exposing them to her weirdness.

Except Jericho. She had been 100 percent herself with him, and it had not gone well.

But who cared.

She was done. She was tired.

"I figured I should spend Christmas with all of you. So here I am."

"You don't have any presents here," her dad said. "I was planning on mailing them."

"It's fine, Dad. I don't really need any presents. And you won't have to mail them, because I'm not leaving."

"Well, that's a good thing."

She looked awkwardly at her dad's girlfriend.

Lucinda Maxfield was supernaturally beautiful. But smooth like a doll, and a bit unapproachable in Honey's opinion. Though the other woman had warmed a lot recently.

"It's good to have you here, Honey," she said.

"Thanks."

She still didn't really know how to interact with her.

It was Jackson who looked at her with the hardest eyes.

And she chose to ignore him.

Instead, she helped herself to the pastries that were set out and took her position around the tree while the others began to open gifts.

"And do you care to give a full accounting for your whereabouts?" Jackson said, succumbing to sit beside her.

"No," she said.

"You were going to leave?"

"I was," she said.

But you didn't. "I didn't."

"But you've been gone."

"Well, I got stuck in the snow."

"Dad mentioned something about that. He mentioned that you and Jericho stayed in…a cabin?"

"I mean, it was a massive vacation rental. But yes."

"I see," he said.

"But I also heard that you were staying with Jericho while he dealt with the Daltons."

"Things change." She sniffed.

"What exactly changed?"

"I didn't want to stay with him anymore?"

"Why?"

"I don't see how that's any of your business," she said.

"You have had the biggest crush on him for as long as I can remember," Jackson said.

Honey's mouth dropped open as a mortified blush spread over her face. She had been prepared to own this and shock them all, and they'd known she had feelings for him! "Now that's not fair..."

"Look, just tell me if I have to go kill him or not."

"I don't want you to kill him," she said, stamping her foot.

"Who are we killing?" Creed asked.

That seemed to get her father's attention too.

"I'm trying to find out about killing Jericho."

"You are not killing him," Honey said.

"Why?" Creed asked.

"Because she's upset about something," Jackson said.

"And?" Creed asked, his tone getting dangerous.

Cricket punched Jackson in the arm. "What is your problem? If you're going to interrogate your sister, at least do it privately. Don't make a dick out of yourself in public."

It was especially funny coming from a woman who was roundly pregnant.

"I'm not being a dick," Jackson said. "I'm trying to figure out if my best friend did something to her. Because I will kill him."

"On what grounds?" Cricket asked, eyeing him closely.

"She's twenty-two."

"And?" Cricket asked, squarely in the same age bracket.

"She's…inexperienced."

Cricket narrowed her eyes. "And?"

"He's my best friend," Jackson said, pointing at Cricket as if that ended things completely.

"Fine. Something happened between myself and Jericho."

That earned her a shocked gasp, and she decided that was pretty satisfying. "And I'm upset about it. But so what? I'm allowed to be upset. You can't protect me from every bad feeling, any more than you can just order me not to have them. I'm going to live life."

"He didn't need to help you do it," Creed said.

"I wanted him to," Honey said. "Because I love him. Okay?" She was saying it. Saying it all. If she'd gotten one gift from Jericho over this time, it hadn't been losing her virginity or the winery. It had been this. This path to honesty. To figuring out that she wanted to share her emotions, whether it made others comfortable or not. To having the confidence to be true to herself, no matter what.

"I don't have a crush on him. I am in love with him. And he can't handle it. That's fine, it wouldn't be my problem, except that I'm in love with him, so it de facto becomes my problem, because he hasn't sorted his shit out yet. But I love him. And that's just... It's the way it is. I don't need any of you getting up in my grill and meddling. I don't need any of you to tell me not to be upset. Because I am. I'm upset. And I'm just... I'm going to be upset for a while. That's how it is."

"Honey, he should never have..."

"He should never what? No, I'm part of this. It wasn't him. It was me too. I wanted it. I want him. And everybody needs to listen to me and to what I want for a minute. Because I have done a pretty terrible job of making myself seen these last few years of my life, and I'm over it. I want him. I want to own the winery. I'm not a kid. I'm a woman. And I want to be treated like one."

"Nobody means to treat you like a kid..."

"No, you do. Because it makes you more comfortable. And I have been all about making sure that you guys are as comfortable as possible. And I'm done with it. So yeah, I'm hurt. And I'm going to be hurt for a little while. And maybe I'm going to have to navigate working with Jericho while I also sort through dealing with the fact that he broke my heart. But I have to deal with it. Not you. You don't get to go and punch him in the face just to make yourselves feel better. Because that's all it would be."

"I aim to kill him," Jackson said, which earned him another slug from his wife.

"Your sister just told you not to. So who would you be doing it for?"

"Me," Creed and Jackson said together.

"I am sorry," her dad said slowly, shaking his head. "I haven't stopped thinking about what you said about your mother's funeral. Not since you mentioned that to me last night. I knew I'd handled that badly, but honestly… I had not been able to remember it. So much of those days are a blur."

"It affected us all," Creed said, taking a step closer to her. "We should have recognized you needed more."

"No, you were grieving too," Honey said.

"Yeah, of course we were," Jackson said.

"None of us were ready to lose her. But you were thirteen."

"I didn't handle it well, Honey, and I'm just so sorry," her dad said.

"Dad, I don't need you to apologize to me."

"But I need to," he said. "Your tears hurt me, Honey. And I couldn't stand them. I tried to make myself comfortable, you're right. And I never meant to teach you to do that for the whole rest of your life. That's not what I wanted. I don't want you to be hurt by Jericho. It makes me angry enough to go ask him how the hell he could betray me after I did so much for him. But you're right. It was your choice. And it's your choice what you do going forward. Because heartbreak happens. It just does. And there's nothing anyone can do to shield us from it. I wish I could, but I didn't protect you when it mattered most, so I have no right to go meddling in your business now."

"But you did protect me, Dad. You loved me, and you gave me a place to live. You didn't fail me across the board just because I have some issues. We all have issues."

At this, Lucinda laughed. "Yes, we really do."

Emerson raised her glass, and next to her, so did her husband Holden. "Amen," Emerson said.

"I don't know what any of you are talking about," Wren said. "I am a shining example of being perfectly adjusted."

"Yeah, your choice of husband says otherwise," Emerson pointed out.

"What's wrong with Creed?"

"It's not Creed himself," Emerson said. "It's the fact that you literally thought you hated him so much you wanted to tear his throat out with your teeth before you hooked up with him."

Creed shrugged. "She does have a point. That's not exactly the act of a well-balanced person."

"You're all terrible."

But they weren't. They were her family. And it was a little bit of a strange mess. And so was she. And she wasn't entirely comfortable here still. But… She would be. Because she would figure it out. She wasn't afraid of trying and failing. She wasn't afraid to ask for what she wanted.

She had done it, and it had backfired spectacularly. But now there was basically nowhere left to go.

She was just going to survive it, because she had to.

And that was—in the middle of a very bad Christmas—perhaps the brightest revelation of all.

When he arrived at Christmas breakfast without Honey, he got a lot of follow-up questions.

"She had to go back home," he said.

And that was how he fended off every single one of them.

They had only been his family for two seconds. They didn't get to ask questions. They didn't get to pass judgment on him. Even though he was neck-deep in passing judgment on himself. He just kept seeing Honey's face in his mind's eye. The way that she was crying.

Yeah. He was a total dick.

"How are you finding the family?"

McKenna sidled up beside him, a big gooey cinnamon roll in hand.

"Just fine."

"You seem…like you aren't sure about all this."

"I'm not," he said.

She nodded. "I get that. I do. You know, I was just going to try to get money out of Hank." She tore a strip off the cinnamon roll and took a bite of it.

"I don't need his money."

"Well, nice for you. I sure did. I was homeless when I came here. Pretty much hated everyone and everything. I did a lot of rough living. I was just… I was really angry at the world. And it was really something meeting Grant, who experienced… Just such a sad loss. And yet he was him. Just unfailingly him. He's a really good man. I don't know that I was a good person when I showed up. I just wanted to get what I felt like Hank owed me. And go on my way. But in the end I got something a lot more."

"You sound like a holiday commercial for plastic wrap."

"Are they particularly sappy?"

"Every holiday commercial is particularly sappy."

"Well, sorry I sound like an ad. I don't intend to. But I don't want you to just never come back."

"Why?"

"Because we all need somebody. I really needed this family. I didn't know it. And I really needed Grant."

"And why mention that?"

"Because I don't want you to let Honey get away either. I think you love her."

"Yeah, because you've known me for twelve hours?"

"Maybe that's how being your sister works. I don't know. Maybe I just sense it."

"So, you're psychic?"

"Maybe I'm just not a dumbass."

"Right. Okay." He started to move away from her, but she followed him. Was this what having a little sister was like? He couldn't say that he loved it.

"I think you love her, and I think you're letting your baggage get in the way. I don't think she just randomly left."

"So what? So what if something happened?"

"I think it's sad. Because I think she's a sweetheart. And I think you're probably a decent guy underneath all your rage at the unfairness of life."

"Look, you've been through some stuff," he said. "Haven't you ever just felt like love was too hard? Like it was too much work?" He shouldn't have asked for that. Because it pushed at tender places inside of his soul that he didn't want to acknowledge. Things he never wanted to deal with.

"Sure," she said. "And loving Grant wasn't simple. Because he had to make room in his heart for me, because he… He'd been in love with someone else before. And she was a really neat woman. She changed him. Into the man who I needed. The man who could love me. Always be grateful to her for that. But that didn't make our road easy, and yeah, I wondered if it was worth it. And why I had to work so hard for love. But you know… In the end, it's worth it. In the end it gives more than it takes."

"Unless it takes everything."

"Are you really afraid of love being hard work? Or are you afraid of losing it? Because I have to tell you, I'm pretty sure it's the second one. And it seems to me that you've already lost her."

"I…"

"The fact that it's on your terms doesn't make it any different."

And he didn't know how to argue with that. Didn't know what to say. Because yeah, he was sitting there, and he didn't have Honey.

He didn't have her.

The realization hit him with the force of a ton of bricks.

She had said that she loved him and he chased her away.

And she was…

He never wanted that. That domestic life, because it reminded him of dark houses and struggle. Of illness.

But not Honey.

She was something else. She was a generic imagining of what marriage might be like. Of what love might be like. She was her. Utterly and uniquely her, and she had been brave enough to tell him how she felt and he had pushed her away.

Did he love her?

Yeah, he already did. He had for a long time, and he hadn't known what to do about it. And he could see himself suddenly, clearly. A man at the top of his game, at the top of the world. Rich as fuck, but poor where it counted. He had come to his family to prove how together he was, but he wasn't together. He just happened to own a lot of shit. That wasn't the same as being successful. He didn't know how to love.

He didn't know how to accept the love of the beautiful woman he had taken to bed last night. He didn't know... You know how. You just got too selfish. Too scared to do it.

The truth stretched before him, undeniable, like the clear harsh light of the sun. And he didn't want to look directly at it. Because it burned him, that truth. That he was nothing. That he had nothing. That he would trade every ounce of success for a week in a cabin with her. No electricity, just Honey to keep him warm.

Right then he felt bankrupt. As rich and successful as he'd ever been, and useless with it.

"Are you having a revelation?" McKenna asked.

"You know," he said. "Having a sister really is overrated."

"It's a weird thing, to go from looking out for yourself to having a whole bunch of people look out for you. Believe me, I get it. But in the end it's worth it."

"So what do I do?"

"It's not easy. But something my husband did... All those years ago and we were working out our stuff, it has stuck with me ever since. It's informed a lot of what I've done, and the ways that I worked out my own issues. Because it's ongoing. I love Grant more than anything in the world, but I'm still scarred from the way that I grew up. And sometimes I lash out. Sometimes I'm not the best to be around. Sometimes I'm insecure. He used to wear this wedding ring. Around his neck. And it was a symbol. Of his grief more than anything else. And one that he chose to set down. He left it at her grave. And it doesn't mean that all the feelings went away. But it's just that... The act of it. Putting it down. Rather than carrying it. That has stuck with me. So every time an issue from my past comes up, I ask myself... McKenna are you just carrying this around? Are you still holding on to it? Why don't you put it down?"

"And that works?"

"Like I said. Not perfectly. But I can picture myself doing it. And walking away. And being happier for it. Just because the world gave you grief doesn't mean you're obligated to carry it on your back forever."

"I don't want to."

"Then don't. I choose to carry around love in the greater measure. And my arms aren't big enough to hold everything. So, mostly, I try to make room to hold that."

"Still sounds like it's work."

She shrugged. "So is being miserable."

And she had a damn good point. She really did.

"What do I do?"

She smiled and took another bite of that cinnamon roll. "Grovel."

Thirteen

By the time Honey got back to the winery that night, she felt gritty. Tired. She was glad she had persevered through the entire holiday, but she hadn't always been the best company, and… She hadn't minded.

She had spoken her piece. And she had been honest about how she felt, and from her perspective that was some pretty decent growth.

Good for her. She had emotional growth. She did not, however, have the love of her life.

She saw headlights, and her heart stopped.

She looked out the window of her little house, and she stared.

Was it Jericho?

It was a big ass truck.

He would go to the house. He wouldn't come talk to her.

Except he pulled right up out front, and he turned the engine off.

Like he intended to stay a bit.

She paced back and forth for a second, and then she decided to take action.

She flung the door open. "Have you come to cause more damage? Because I warn you, I am not in a space to make stupid men comfortable by minimizing my feelings."

"You sound like my sister," he said.

"Your sister?"

"Yeah. McKenna."

That made something in her chest tighten. "Oh. So that went well."

"Yeah. I'm going to have to see them again another time. Because I realized that I needed to get back here."

"Why?"

"I realized I needed to get back to you."

"Back to me?"

"Yeah," he said. "Because I realized that I was being a coward. You said that you love me and I couldn't handle it. Because it reminded me of grief. You know why I hated Christmas so much? Because it almost made me feel happy. And it gave me this terrible sense that there was joy out there in the world, and all these people were feeling it. And I felt like I was standing on the outside of it. Able to feel just the edges of it. But never the whole thing. Like I could see the light in this dark winter, but I could never really… I can never really stand in it. It reminded me of that. You offering me your love. Like I was standing on the edge of something beautiful but I didn't know how to take it."

"Jericho…"

"I want it. I want all of it. I want you and me and I want to love you. And I want you to show me. And I need you to have all your emotions, Honey. I need them to be as big and bright as Christmas Day. I need them to be bigger and brighter than the sun, because I need to feel them. Because I need… I need that joy. I need more than the darkness."

Her heart expanded, full to bursting. "I need it too," she said, flinging herself into his arms. "I love you."

"You're not even going to make me suffer?"

"We've both suffered enough," she said.

And that was the damned truth. It truly was. They had both suffered enough.

And what he found was that even though it filled his chest, love wasn't heavy. Not really. It wasn't light, but it didn't weigh them down. And it lit up the dark corners of his soul with all the brilliance of midday.

With the promise of Christmas. And joy to the world. But most especially and finally, to him.

They had been caught in the storm, but the biggest storm had been raging inside of him all this time. And now it was like the sun had come out from behind the clouds. And everything was gold.

Gold like Honey.

"I love you," he said. And while he did, he imagined himself setting his fear down on the floor and leaving it there. Dropping bits and pieces of grief, of doubt. Because all he wanted to carry was her. He wanted to fill his arms with her, fill his chest with her. Forever.

"I love you too," she said. "I'm really glad I didn't burn this place to the ground."

"What?"

"You know, just something I considered. When I was furious at you and convinced that I couldn't have everything that I wanted."

"And what do you think now?"

"That I'll take everything I want and then some. Because why should we settle? That's what we've been doing. Deciding that people like us—who have experienced a measure of tragedy—that we don't get to have the full measure of happiness. But I say we do it. I say we claim it."

"That sounds like a great idea."

And he kissed her. With no doubt or shame, and a whole lot of love.

And he knew that he would be doing it for the rest of his life.

Epilogue

Their whole family was practically a town gathering. Between the Daltons, the Maxfields and the Coopers, Cowboy Wines was absolutely full tonight for Christmas. They had decided in the end to rotate around the Christmas festivities, because it allowed everybody to have the kind of Christmas they loved the most. And no, they didn't do it once a year, they had three Christmases. And everyone was invited.

And when the Daltons hosted, the festivities included the Dodges, Luke and Olivia

Hollister, and hell, they might as well just have invited the whole town.

If there was one thing Honey had learned, really learned in the last few years, it was that love grew to accommodate. To expand around all your joy, all your sorrow. And she was sure that their joy was only going to expand more as they added to their family. She hadn't told Jericho yet.

But she would. Christmas morning.

She smiled thinking of the onesie wrapped beneath the tree.

And she felt tears sting her eyes. Just for a moment.

As she thought of the ones they wouldn't have with them for the birth of their first child.

And then she realized, with absolute certainty. But they did have them. In their hearts. Always. Because all the people they'd lost, whether it was her and Jericho or even the members of the Dalton family... Their losses had brought them to this place. Of loving with fierce abandon. Of loving as if it was the most important thing on earth. The only thing on earth.

Because it was.

She looked over at her husband, and she smiled.

She was quite certain that their love was the biggest and brightest of all.

And the next morning when he took that small box from beneath the tree and unwrapped it, it was a moment shared just between the two of them.

"You're kidding me," he said, his eyes filled with wonder. Joy. And she realized that all those years before, she had never seen him look quite like that.

"I'm very serious. And very happy. I hope you are too."

"I didn't have a father growing up," he said, his voice sounding strangled. "And I never imagined I'd be one. I didn't think that I would ever get to be so damned blessed."

"We both are. We both are."

And he kissed her. In that way that she had grown to love so very much. That way that meant forever. That way that always reminded her of Christmas and field guides to birds and love.

Always and forever love.

* * * * *